Little Poets

Edited By Sarah Washer

First published in Great Britian in 2016 by:

Coltsfoot Drive
Peterborough
PE2 9BF
Telephone: 01733 890066
Website: www.youngwriters.co.uk

All Rights Reserved
Book Design by Tim Christian
© Copyright Contributors 2016
SB ISBN 978-1-78624-262-4
Printed and bound in the UK by BookPrintingUK
Website: www.bookprintinguk.com
YB0270H

Foreword

Young Writers was established in 1991 with the aim of encouraging writing skills in young people and giving them the opportunity to see their work in print. Poetry is a wonderful way to introduce young children to the idea of rhyme and rhythm and helps learning and development of communication, language and literacy skills.

'My First Poem' was created to introduce nursery and preschool children to this wonderful world of poetry. They were given a template to fill in with their own words, creating a poem that was all about them.

We are proud to present the resulting collection of personal and touching poems in this anthology, which can be treasured for years to come.

Jenni Bannister
Editorial Manager

Contents

Blue Giraffe Childcare, Walsall

Macie Grace Etherington (3)	1
Olly Barratt (3)	2
Aidan Hitchock (3)	3
Olly Dennis Marston (3)	4
Jacob Harrison Ferrie (4)	5
Alex Reynolds (2)	6
Eliza Jackson (3)	7
Jayden Kanjere (4)	8
Zach Hammond (3)	9
Mollie Mae Stuart Walter (3)	10
Oscar Moore (4)	11
Elvie Johnson (3)	12
Maisy Watts (4)	13
Charley Styler Morgan (3)	14
Ben Gillot (4)	15

Catherine House Day Nursery School, London

Jahnyah Nicely (4)	16
Georgia Rose Maini Gadhok (4)	17
Ava-Monét Oduro (4)	18
Kayla Sekeroglu (4)	19
George Edward Trim (4)	20
Amelie Simone Cauwenbergh (4)	21
Matilda Annie Bateup (4)	22
Rosie Martin (4)	23
Sienna Marianne Ford-Miah (4)	24

Elgin Nursery, Croydon

Yash Kurdekar (3)	25
Elijah Jireh Asiimwe (3)	26
Joshua Christopher Suckling (3)	27
Rowan Harry (3)	28
Nathaniel Samuel (3)	29
Tany-Ann Tony (3)	30
Elwin Charles (3)	31
Lucas Friesenegger (4)	32

Fun Frogs Day Nursery, Wilmslow

Lillyana Crow (3)	33
Lola Rose Blunt (4)	34
Libbie Rose Tomlinson (4)	35
Holly Stephenson (4)	36
Orla Lomas (3)	37
Ethan Beran (3)	38
William Jacob Buchanan (3)	39
Bella Raine Child (4)	40
Amelia-Grace Edwards (3)	41
George Roberts-Gubb (3)	42
Bethan Watts (3)	43
Maddison Faith Ella Wilson (3)	44
Emily Grace Doolan (4)	45
Harriet Gibbons (3)	46
Taylor Gaffney (4)	47
Eleanor Frances Little (3)	48
Lily Stewart-Douglas (4)	49
Amy Lake (3)	50
George Prideaux (3)	51

Gershwin Park Day Nursery School, Witham

Lilah Glasby (3)	52
Jamie Jonathan Robert Buttress (3)	53
Tyler Hawthorne (3)	54
Samuel Frederick Baxter (4)	55
Daan Verstraete (3)	56
Noah Barker (3)	57
Ava Williams (3)	58
Erin Dymock (2)	59
Chloe McColm (4)	60
Katie McColm (3)	61
Milla Elizabeth Ding (3)	62

Honeypot Day Nursery & Preschool, Spalding

Charlie Dunmore (4)	63
Wojciech Jasnikowski (4)	64
Dominic Joshua Palmer (4)	65
Florence Brown (3)	66
Jaxon Taplin (4)	67
Millie Rose Elderkin (4)	68
Susannah Poll (3)	69
Bonnie Beadle-Wright (3)	70
Abbi Johnson (3)	71
Ruby Mae Frith (3)	72
Matilda Motley-Webber (3)	73
Alfie Desmond (3)	74
Marley Bycraft (4)	75

Joel Nursery, London

Bianca Cancela (3)	76
Tybias Sinclair (3)	77
Kaila-Marie Smith-Weekes (4)	78
Balma Mballta (3)	79
Aiden Dean Patel (2)	80

Kenton Day Nursery, Harrow

Aryan Patel (4)	81
Rohan Shah (3)	82
Aaheli Roy (3)	83
Mehar Jain (3)	84
Riana Ragel (3)	85
Kanaya Samani (3)	86

Ladybird Forest Preschool, Bedford

Madeleine Floyd (3)	87
Lucas Hickman (3)	88
Zoe Harding (4)	89
Scarlett Stocker (2)	90
Dylan Sylvester (3)	91
Evie Isabella Sheridan (3)	92
Isabel Grace McCrindle (3)	93
Lavinia Jean Waller (4)	94
Jackson Gray Amis (3)	95
Grace Marabese (2)	96
Eliza Wilkinson (3)	97
Evie Spencer (3)	98
Herbie Paterson (4)	99
Larni Rose Jones (4)	100
Jasper Doohan (4)	101

Little Acorns Nursery, Leicester

Joshua Tomlinson	102
Vikram Sahdev (3)	103
Dilraj Sahdev (4)	104
Diiya Bharakhda (3)	105
Jasper Jan Anderson (3)	106
Langelihle Rishi Booi (2)	107
Amar Singh Ruprai (3)	108
Elisha Hope Alice Matu (4)	109
Poppy Rhodes	110
Billy Beau Brandreth (3)	111

Theo Culverwell 112
Harveer Singh Loyal (3) 113
Leonard John Trevelyan Miller (2) 114
Reuben Louis Hampson-Goodyear (3) 115
Imogen Fearne Burrows (3) 116

Little Cherubs Day Nursery, Bromley

Samantha Grace De Villiers (4) 117
Malaika Khoso (2) 118
Gezal Mehdipour (3) 119
Grace Garatti-Lloyd (3) 120
Lacey-Jayne Ellis (3) 121
Abbie Wood (3) 122
Leo Harriss (3) 123
Ruby Slatter (3) 124
Elisa Wong (4) 125
Maxwell Hawker (4) 126
Charlie Parker (4) 127

Little Explorers Day Nursery, Leicester

Andrea Reischig (2) 128
Mia Bella Puna (3) 129
Khaleesi Allsop (2) 130
Kayleigh Campbell (3) 131
Arlo Zachary Jallands (4) 132
William Neilson (3) 133
Sasha Needham (2) 134

Patacake Day Nursery, Cambridge

Lucie Ada Edme-Brenot (4) 135
Ari Smith Posner (4) 136

Red Balloon Day Nursery, Cobham

Prudence Millie Mallindine (4) 137
Elwood Tiernan (4) 138
Evie Willow Cook 139
Liya Shuja 140
Alice Florence Berry (3) 141
Holly Price (3) 142
Benjamin Cobden (3) 143
Aaron Beardmore (3) 144
Ischia Heathfield (4) 145

Roberts Day Nursery, Portsmouth

Amber Šutka (4) 146
McKenzie Hudson (4) 147
Cobie Marshall (3) 148
Abigail Walton (3) 149
Esmee Mitchell-Farmer (2) 150
Charlie Spratt (3) 151
Cherrish Clarke (4) 152
Ben Mendy (3) 153
India Lewis-Connock (4) 154
Amara Egwuatu (3) 155
Logun Elston (4) 156
Freddie Harvey (3) 157
Emily Coles (3) 158
Lily Summer Ruddy (3) 159
Melah Bah (3) 160
Lucja Pioro (3) 161
Sade-Nia Tull (4) 162
Billy Burgess (3) 163
Tiegan Dobson (3) 164
Maggie May Stewart (3) 165
Ocean-Lea Morey (4) 166

School House Nursery, Sandwich

Evie Grace Hayes (4)	167
Skye Gibbons (3)	168

Stepping Stones Private Day Nursery, Pershore

Katie James (4)	169
Callum Webb (3)	170
Morgan Archer-Smith (3)	171
Maddison Young (3)	172
Edward George Dorrell (3)	173
Nicole Amelia Price (2)	174

Teddies Southampton, Southampton

Paula Gomez (3)	175
Samuel Burch (4)	176
Jay Salvi (3)	177
Shaeley Geddes (3)	178
Zack Day (4)	179
Ava Conway (3)	180
Sophie Ulumma-Anusionwu (4)	181
Isobelle Lang (3)	182
Riley Atterbury (4)	183
Amelia Stone (3)	184
Anoop Singh (3)	185
Isabella Tang (3)	186
Alissa Oswald (4)	187
Emily Grace Mellors (4)	188
Poppy June Cochrane (3)	189
Imelda Samways (4)	190
Jack Moverley (4)	191
Kaj Hill (3)	192
Jarmal Makawa (3)	193
Esmé Dornan (4)	194
Robyn Hayward (4)	195
Amelia Louise Mullins (3)	196
Zachariya Uddin (3)	197
Lucas William Sargent (4)	198
Arianna Gbadamosi (4)	199

Tiddlywinks Nursery, Manchester

Raiaan Rafiq (3)	200
Jenson Mansell (4)	201
Myla Clyne (3)	202
Erin Thackeray (4)	203
Harrison Fisher (3)	204
Aniella Dalbin (3)	205
Kale Lamey-McArthur (3)	206
Eva Walklett (3)	207
Eric McCormick (3)	208

The Poems

My First Poem

My name is Macie and I go to preschool,
My best friend is Eliza, who is really cool.
I watch Peppa Pig on TV,
Playing with Eliza is lots of fun for me.
I just love pizza to eat,
And sometimes ice cream for a treat.
Brown is a colour I like a lot,
My shoes are the best present I ever got.
My favourite person is Baillee, who is a gem,
So this, my first poem, is just for them!

Macie Grace Etherington (3)

Blue Giraffe Childcare, Walsall

My First Poem

My name is Olly and I go to preschool,
My best friend is Jacob, who is really cool.
I watch In the Night Garden on TV,
Playing on the motorbike is lots of fun for me.
I just love cheese to eat,
And sometimes sweets for a treat.
Red is a colour I like a lot,
My Spider-Man is the best present I ever got.
My favourite person is Mommy, who is a gem,
So this, my first poem, is just for them!

Olly Barratt (3)
Blue Giraffe Childcare, Walsall

My First Poem

My name is **Aidan** and I go to preschool,
My best friend is **Olly**, who is really cool.
I watch **racing cars** on TV,
Playing **with Bumblebee** is lots of fun for me.
I just love **sandwiches** to eat,
And sometimes **sweeties** for a treat.
Red is a colour I like a lot,
My **train table** is the best present I ever got.
My favourite person is **Olly**, who is a gem,
So this, my first poem, is just for them!

Aidan Hitchock (3)

Blue Giraffe Childcare, Walsall

My First Poem

My name is Olly and I go to preschool,
My best friend is Macie, who is really cool.
I watch superheroes on TV,
Playing with cars is lots of fun for me.
I just love beans to eat,
And sometimes cake for a treat.
Red is a colour I like a lot,
My Thomas is the best present I ever got.
My favourite person is Mommy, who is a gem,
So this, my first poem, is just for them!

Olly Dennis Marston (3)
Blue Giraffe Childcare, Walsall

My First Poem

My name is **Jacob** and I go to preschool,
My best friend is **Olly**, who is really cool.
I watch **Avengers** on TV,
Playing **ball** is lots of fun for me.
I just love **ribs** to eat,
And sometimes **sweets** for a treat.
Orange and black are colours I like a lot,
My **sword** is the best present I ever got.
My favourite people are **Mommy, Daddy and Joshy**, who are gems,
So this, my first poem, is just for them!

Jacob Harrison Ferrie (4)

Blue Giraffe Childcare, Walsall

My First Poem

My name is **Alex** and I go to preschool,
My best friends are **Mommy and Daddy**, who are really cool.
I watch **Peppa Pig** on TV,
Playing **with dinosaurs** is lots of fun for me.
I just love **food** to eat,
And sometimes **chocolate mousse** for a treat.
Orange and red are colours I like a lot,
My **helmet** is the best present I ever got.
My favourite person is **Daddy**, who is a gem,
So this, my first poem, is just for them!

Alex Reynolds (2)
Blue Giraffe Childcare, Walsall

My First Poem

My name is **Eliza** and I go to preschool,
My best friend is **Macie**, who is really cool.
I watch **Frozen** on TV,
Playing **with toys** is lots of fun for me.
I just love **potato and pie** to eat,
And sometimes **sweeties** for a treat.
Black is a colour I like a lot,
My **zebra** is the best present I ever got.
My favourite person is **Mommy**, who is a gem,
So this, my first poem, is just for them!

Eliza Jackson (3)

Blue Giraffe Childcare, Walsall

My First Poem

My name is Jayden and I go to preschool,
My best friend is Joshua, who is really cool.
I watch Cars on TV,
Playing with toys is lots of fun for me.
I just love porridge to eat,
And sometimes ice cream for a treat.
Yellow is a colour I like a lot,
My Lightning McQueen is the best present I ever got.
My favourite person is Percy, who is a gem,
So this, my first poem, is just for them!

Jayden Kanjere (4)
Blue Giraffe Childcare, Walsall

My First Poem

My name is **Zach** and I go to preschool,
My best friend is **Charlie**, who is really cool.
I watch **dinosaurs** on TV,
Playing **with my cars** is lots of fun for me.
I just love **chicken** to eat,
And sometimes **Weetabix** for a treat.
Purple is a colour I like a lot,
My **games** are the best presents I ever got.
My favourite people are **Mommy and Daddy**, who are gems,
So this, my first poem, is just for them!

Zach Hammond (3)

Blue Giraffe Childcare, Walsall

My First Poem

My name is Mollie and I go to preschool,
My best friend is Eliza, who is really cool.
I watch CBeebies on TV,
Playing cars is lots of fun for me.
I just love sausages to eat,
And sometimes chocolate for a treat.
Red is a colour I like a lot,
My baby is the best present I ever got.
My favourite person is my mommy, who is a gem,
So this, my first poem, is just for them!

Mollie Mae Stuart Walter (3)
Blue Giraffe Childcare, Walsall

My First Poem

My name is Oscar and I go to preschool,
My best friend is Zach, who is really cool.
I watch PAW Patrol on TV,
Playing with my toys is lots of fun for me.
I just love chips to eat,
And sometimes I get PAW Patrol stickers for a treat.
Red is a colour I like a lot,
My PAW Patrol Rubble is the best present I ever got.
My favourite person is Zach, who is a gem,
So this, my first poem, is just for them!

Oscar Moore (4)

Blue Giraffe Childcare, Walsall

My First Poem

My name is Elvie and I go to preschool,
My best friend is Taya, who is really cool.
I watch Peppa Pig on TV,
Playing cars is lots of fun for me.
I just love nuggets to eat,
And sometimes sweets for a treat.
Pink is a colour I like a lot,
My bag is the best present I ever got.
My favourite person is Mommy, who is a gem,
So this, my first poem, is just for them!

Elvie Johnson (3)
Blue Giraffe Childcare, Walsall

My First Poem

My name is **Maisy** and I go to preschool,
My best friend is **Ben**, who is really cool.
I watch **CBeebies** on TV,
Playing **with my teddy** is lots of fun for me.
I just love **cheese on toast** to eat,
And sometimes **sweets** for a treat.
Blue is a colour I like a lot,
My **Mickey Mouse** is the best present I ever got.
My favourite person is **Mommy**, who is a gem,
So this, my first poem, is just for them!

Maisy Watts (4)

Blue Giraffe Childcare, Walsall

My First Poem

My name is **Charley** and I go to preschool,
My best friend is **Olly**, who is really cool.
I watch **Jake and the Never Land Pirates** on TV,
Playing **with toys** is lots of fun for me.
I just love **pizza** to eat,
And sometimes **sweets** for a treat.
Blue is a colour I like a lot,
My **hungry pig** is the best present I ever got.
My favourite person is **Mommy**, who is a gem,
So this, my first poem, is just for them!

Charley Styler Morgan (3)
Blue Giraffe Childcare, Walsall

My First Poem

My name is Ben and I go to preschool,
My best friend is Mommy, who is really cool.
I watch CBeebies on TV,
Playing with Maisy is lots of fun for me.
I just love vegetable soup to eat,
And sometimes cakes for a treat.
Yellow, purple and pink are colours I like a lot,
My Frozen blanket is the best present I ever got.
My favourite person is Mommy, who is a gem,
So this, my first poem, is just for them!

Ben Gillot (4)

Blue Giraffe Childcare, Walsall

My First Poem

My name is Jahnyah and I go to preschool,
My best friend is Maya, who is really cool.
I watch Peppa Pig on TV,
Playing with Neriah is lots of fun for me.
I just love rice to eat,
And sometimes chocolate for a treat.
Pink is a colour I like a lot,
My bike is the best present I ever got.
My favourite person is Mummy, who is a gem,
So this, my first poem, is just for them!

Jahnyah Nicely (4)
Catherine House Day Nursery School, London

My First Poem

My name is Georgia and I go to preschool,
My best friend is Amelie, who is really cool.
I watch Frozen on TV,
Playing with toys is lots of fun for me.
I just love cucumber to eat,
And sometimes chocolate for a treat.
Purple is a colour I like a lot,
My ball is the best present I ever got.
My favourite person is Jemima, who is a gem,
So this, my first poem, is just for them!

Georgia Rose Maini Gadhok (4)

Catherine House Day Nursery School, London

My First Poem

My name is Ava-Monét and I go to preschool,
My best friend is Maya, who is really cool.
I watch My Little Pony on TV,
Playing with toys is lots of fun for me.
I just love macaroni cheese to eat,
And sometimes sweets for a treat.
Yellow is a colour I like a lot,
My book is the best present I ever got.
My favourite person is Jahnyah, who is a gem,
So this, my first poem, is just for them!

Ava-Monét Oduro (4)
Catherine House Day Nursery School, London

My First Poem

My name is **Kayla** and I go to preschool,
My best friend is **Isadora**, who is really cool.
I watch **Peppa Pig** on TV,
Playing **in the home corner** is lots of fun for me.
I just love **macaroni cheese** to eat,
And sometimes **biscuits** for a treat.
Pink is a colour I like a lot,
My **teddy bear** is the best present I ever got.
My favourite person is **Isadora**, who is a gem,
So this, my first poem, is just for them!

Kayla Sekeroglu (4)
Catherine House Day Nursery School, London

My First Poem

My name is George and I go to preschool,
My best friend is Mummy, who is really cool.
I watch Dinopaws on TV,
Playing with the train tracks is lots of fun for me.
I just love scrambled egg to eat,
And sometimes ice cream for a treat.
Blue is a colour I like a lot,
My rocket is the best present I ever got.
My favourite person is Mummy, who is a gem,
So this, my first poem, is just for them!

George Edward Trim (4)
Catherine House Day Nursery School, London

My First Poem

My name is **Amelie** and I go to preschool,
My best friend is **Isadora**, who is really cool.
I watch **Milkshake** on TV,
Playing **on the piano** is lots of fun for me.
I just love **fish and chips** to eat,
And sometimes **apples** for a treat.
Purple is a colour I like a lot,
My **cat bag** is the best present I ever got.
My favourite person is **Mummy**, who is a gem,
So this, my first poem, is just for them!

Amelie Simone Cauwenbergh (4)

Catherine House Day Nursery School, London

My First Poem

My name is Matilda and I go to preschool,
My best friend is Eliza, who is really cool.
I watch Peppa Pig on TV,
Playing games is lots of fun for me.
I just love fish and chips to eat,
And sometimes crisps for a treat.
Purple is a colour I like a lot,
My My Little Pony is the best present I ever got.
My favourite person is Grandad, who is a gem,
So this, my first poem, is just for them!

Matilda Annie Bateup (4)

Catherine House Day Nursery School, London

My First Poem

My name is **Rosie** and I go to preschool,
My best friend is **Lucas**, who is really cool.
I watch **Whisper** on TV,
Playing **with dolls** is lots of fun for me.
I just love **broccoli and carrots** to eat,
And sometimes **lollies** for a treat.
Purple is a colour I like a lot,
My **pens** are the best present I ever got.
My favourite person is **Mummy**, who is a gem,
So this, my first poem, is just for them!

Rosie Martin (4)

Catherine House Day Nursery School, London

My First Poem

My name is Sienna and I go to preschool,
My best friend is Eliza, who is really cool.
I watch Ladybug on TV,
Playing games is lots of fun for me.
I just love fish and chips to eat,
And sometimes crisps for a treat.
Black is a colour I like a lot,
My My Little Pony is the best present I ever got.
My favourite person is my brother, who is a gem,
So this, my first poem, is just for them!

Sienna Marianne Ford-Miah (4)
Catherine House Day Nursery School, London

My First Poem

My name is **Yash** and I go to preschool,
My best friend is **Jagoda**, who is really cool.
I watch **Toy Story** on TV,
Playing **Magnetix** is lots of fun for me.
I just love **a burger** to eat,
And sometimes **ice cream** for a treat.
Red is a colour I like a lot,
My **Minion** is the best present I ever got.
My favourite person is **Nathaniel**, who is a gem,
So this, my first poem, is just for them!

Yash Kurdekar (3)

Elgin Nursery, Croydon

My First Poem

My name is **Elijah** and I go to preschool,
My best friend is **Sreemaa**, who is really cool.
I watch **football** on TV,
Playing **with the Magnetix** is lots of fun for me.
I just love **pasta** to eat,
And sometimes **a Kinder egg** for a treat.
Orange is a colour I like a lot,
My **car** is the best present I ever got.
My favourite person is **Mummy**, who is a gem,
So this, my first poem, is just for them!

Elijah Jireh Asiimwe (3)

Elgin Nursery, Croydon

My First Poem

My name is Joshua and I go to preschool,
My best friend is Lucas, who is really cool.
I watch PAW Patrol on TV,
Playing with the Mega Bloks is lots of fun for me.
I just love a sandwich to eat,
And sometimes a sweetie for a treat.
Green is a colour I like a lot,
My drum is the best present I ever got.
My favourite person is Emilia, who is a gem,
So this, my first poem, is just for them!

Joshua Christopher Suckling (3)

Elgin Nursery, Croydon

My First Poem

My name is **Rowan** and I go to preschool,
My best friend is **Georgie**, who is really cool.
I watch **Peppa Pig** on TV,
Playing **with Magnetix** is lots of fun for me.
I just love **fish fingers** to eat,
And sometimes **crisps** for a treat.
Blue is a colour I like a lot,
My **train** is the best present I ever got.
My favourite person is **Laurie**, who is a gem,
So this, my first poem, is just for them!

Rowan Harry (3)
Elgin Nursery, Croydon

My First Poem

My name is **Nathaniel** and I go to preschool,
My best friend is **Neriah**, who is really cool.
I watch **Spider-Man** on TV,
Playing **with cars** is lots of fun for me.
I just love **chicken** to eat,
And sometimes **cake** for a treat.
Red is a colour I like a lot,
My **ball** is the best present I ever got.
My favourite person is **Mummy**, who is a gem,
So this, my first poem, is just for them!

Nathaniel Samuel (3)

Elgin Nursery, Croydon

My First Poem

My name is **Tany-Ann** and I go to preschool,
My best friend is **Elwin**, who is really cool.
I watch **Sofia** on TV,
Playing **with Lego** is lots of fun for me.
I just love **chicken** to eat,
And sometimes **an apple** for a treat.
Yellow is a colour I like a lot,
My **Minion** is the best present I ever got.
My favourite person is **Tony**, who is a gem,
So this, my first poem, is just for them!

Tany-Ann Tony (3)
Elgin Nursery, Croydon

My First Poem

My name is **Elwin** and I go to preschool,
My best friend is **Tany**, who is really cool.
I watch **PAW Patrol** on TV,
Playing **with Lego** is lots of fun for me.
I just love **vegetables** to eat,
And sometimes **a biscuit** for a treat.
Blue is a colour I like a lot,
My **Chase** is the best present I ever got.
My favourite person is **Akka**, who is a gem,
So this, my first poem, is just for them!

Elwin Charles (3)

Elgin Nursery, Croydon

My First Poem

My name is Lucas and I go to preschool,
My best friend is Sonam, who is really cool.
I watch PAW Patrol on TV,
Playing with trains is lots of fun for me.
I just love pancakes to eat,
And sometimes sweeties for a treat.
Orange is a colour I like a lot,
My tube train is the best present I ever got.
My favourite person is Georgie, who is a gem,
So this, my first poem, is just for them!

Lucas Friesenegger (4)
Elgin Nursery, Croydon

My First Poem

My name is **Lillyana** and I go to preschool,
My best friend is **my daddy**, who is really cool.
I watch **SpongeBob** on TV,
Playing **outside** is lots of fun for me.
I just love **fish fingers** to eat,
And sometimes **chocolate** for a treat.
Pink is a colour I like a lot,
My **make-up** is the best present I ever got.
My favourite person is **my mummy**, who is a gem,
So this, my first poem, is just for them!

Lillyana Crow (3)

Fun Frogs Day Nursery, Wilmslow

My First Poem

My name is Lola and I go to preschool,
My best friend is Lucca, who is really cool.
I watch Peppa Pig on TV,
Playing with George Pig is lots of fun for me.
I just love chicken dinner to eat,
And sometimes sweets for a treat.
Pink is a colour I like a lot,
My doll's pram is the best present I ever got.
My favourite person is Alisha, my sister, who is a gem,
So this, my first poem, is just for them!

Lola Rose Blunt (4)

Fun Frogs Day Nursery, Wilmslow

My First Poem

My name is **Libbie** and I go to preschool,
My best friend is **Lily**, who is really cool.
I watch **CBeebies** on TV,
Playing **with Play-Doh** is lots of fun for me.
I just love **mash and sausages** to eat,
And sometimes **sweeties** for a treat.
Pink and blue are colours I like a lot,
My **bike** is the best present I ever got.
My favourite person is **my sister, Brooke**, who is a gem,
So this, my first poem, is just for them!

Libbie Rose Tomlinson (4)

Fun Frogs Day Nursery, Wilmslow

My First Poem

My name is **Holly** and I go to preschool,
My best friend is **my mummy**, who is really cool.
I watch **Peppa Pig** on TV,
Playing **on my scooter** is lots of fun for me.
I just love **broccoli and chips** to eat,
And sometimes **chocolate Smarties** for a treat.
Pink and purple are colours I like a lot,
My **bike** is the best present I ever got.
My favourite person is **my daddy**, who is a gem,
So this, my first poem, is just for them!

Holly Stephenson (4)
Fun Frogs Day Nursery, Wilmslow

My First Poem

My name is **Orla** and I go to preschool,
My best friend is **Lily**, who is really cool.
I watch **SpongeBob** on TV,
Playing **with Play-Doh** is lots of fun for me.
I just love **fish fingers and sauce** to eat,
And sometimes **sweeties** for a treat.
Black is a colour I like a lot,
My **swing** is the best present I ever got.
My favourite person is **my mummy**, who is a gem,
So this, my first poem, is just for them!

Orla Lomas (3)

Fun Frogs Day Nursery, Wilmslow

My First Poem

My name is Ethan and I go to preschool,
My best friend is Oliver, who is really cool.
I watch PAW Patrol on TV,
Playing football is lots of fun for me.
I just love peas to eat,
And sometimes sweets for a treat.
Black is a colour I like a lot,
My rubbish truck is the best present I ever got.
My favourite person is my mummy, who is a gem,
So this, my first poem, is just for them!

Ethan Beran (3)
Fun Frogs Day Nursery, Wilmslow

My First Poem

My name is William and I go to preschool,
My best friend is Luke, who is really cool.
I watch CBeebies on TV,
Playing outside is lots of fun for me.
I just love chicken nuggets to eat,
And sometimes chocolate cake for a treat.
Blue is a colour I like a lot,
My dinosaur is the best present I ever got.
My favourite person is my mummy, who is a gem,
So this, my first poem, is just for them!

William Jacob Buchanan (3)

Fun Frogs Day Nursery, Wilmslow

My First Poem

My name is **Bella** and I go to preschool,
My best friend is **Libbie**, who is really cool.
I watch **PAW Patrol** on TV,
Playing **with my Barbies** is lots of fun for me.
I just love **chicken and chips** to eat,
And sometimes **cheese and onion crisps** for a treat.
Green is a colour I like a lot,
My **Tsum Tsum Squishies** are the best presents I ever got.
My favourite person is **my mummy**, who is a gem,
So this, my first poem, is just for them!

Bella Raine Child (4)

Fun Frogs Day Nursery, Wilmslow

My First Poem

My name is **Amelia-Grace** and I go to preschool,
My best friend is **Max**, who is really cool.
I watch **Thumbelina** on TV,
Playing **in the sand** is lots of fun for me.
I just love **fish fingers, beans and sausage** to eat,
And sometimes **sweets and biscuits** for a treat.
Sparkly pink is a colour I like a lot,
My **Princess Aurora dress** is the best present I ever got.
My favourite person is **my mummy, Kerry**, who is a gem,
So this, my first poem, is just for them!

Amelia-Grace Edwards (3)
Fun Frogs Day Nursery, Wilmslow

My First Poem

My name is George and I go to preschool,
My best friend is Max, who is really cool.
I watch Octonauts on TV,
Playing football is lots of fun for me.
I just love pasta to eat,
And sometimes sweets for a treat.
Blue is a colour I like a lot,
My Captain Barnacles is the best present I ever got.
My favourite person is my daddy, who is a gem,
So this, my first poem, is just for them!

George Roberts-Gubb (3)
Fun Frogs Day Nursery, Wilmslow

My First Poem

My name is **Bethan** and I go to preschool,
My best friend is **Holly**, who is really cool.
I watch **Paddington** on TV,
Playing **pizza, pizza** is lots of fun for me.
I just love **fish fingers and chips** to eat,
And sometimes **biscuits** for a treat.
Pink and purple are colours I like a lot,
My **blue umbrella** is the best present I ever got.
My favourite person is **my mummy**, who is a gem,
So this, my first poem, is just for them!

Bethan Watts (3)

Fun Frogs Day Nursery, Wilmslow

My First Poem

My name is **Maddison** and I go to preschool,
My best friend is **my daddy**, who is really cool.
I watch **Nemo and dinosaurs** on TV,
Playing **with my dolls** is lots of fun for me.
I just love **chicken nuggets** to eat,
And sometimes **chocolate fingers** for a treat.
Red is a colour I like a lot,
My **doll's house** is the best present I ever got.
My favourite person is **my mummy, Ness**, who is a gem,
So this, my first poem, is just for them!

Maddison Faith Ella Wilson (3)
Fun Frogs Day Nursery, Wilmslow

My First Poem

My name is Emily and I go to preschool,
My best friend is Bethan, who is really cool.
I watch Peppa Pig on TV,
Playing with my bricks is lots of fun for me.
I just love spaghetti Bolognese to eat,
And sometimes lollipops for a treat.
Pink is a colour I like a lot,
My doll is the best present I ever got.
My favourite person is my best friend,
Bethan, who is a gem,
So this, my first poem, is just for them!

Emily Grace Doolan (4)

Fun Frogs Day Nursery, Wilmslow

My First Poem

My name is **Harriet** and I go to preschool,
My best friend is **Max**, who is really cool.
I watch **Thomas** on TV,
Playing **with Lego** is lots of fun for me.
I just love **sausages and tomato sauce** to eat,
And sometimes **sweets** for a treat.
Pink is a colour I like a lot,
My **new black sofa** is the best present I ever got.
My favourite person is **my mummy**, who is a gem,
So this, my first poem, is just for them!

Harriet Gibbons (3)

Fun Frogs Day Nursery, Wilmslow

My First Poem

My name is Taylor and I go to preschool,
My best friend is my daddy, who is really cool.
I watch Man City on TV,
Playing football is lots of fun for me.
I just love pasta and cheese to eat,
And sometimes ice cream and chocolate sauce for a treat.
Red is a colour I like a lot,
My Ninja Turtle, Leonardo, is the best present I ever got.
My favourite person is my grandad, Terry, who is a gem,
So this, my first poem, is just for them!

Taylor Gaffney (4)

Fun Frogs Day Nursery, Wilmslow

My First Poem

My name is **Eleanor** and I go to preschool,
My best friend is **Lilia**, who is really cool.
I watch **Ben & Holly** on TV,
Playing **snakes and ladders** is lots of fun for me.
I just love **pasta and ham** to eat,
And sometimes **sweets** for a treat.
Blue is a colour I like a lot,
My **doll's pram** is the best present I ever got.
My favourite person is **my grandad**, who is a gem,
So this, my first poem, is just for them!

Eleanor Frances Little (3)
Fun Frogs Day Nursery, Wilmslow

My First Poem

My name is **Lily** and I go to preschool,
My best friend is **Hallie**, who is really cool.
I watch **Barbie** on TV,
Playing **on my bike** is lots of fun for me.
I just love **pasta** to eat,
And sometimes **sweeties** for a treat.
Pink and purple are colours I like a lot,
My **Barbie doll** is the best present I ever got.
My favourite person is **my daddy**, who is a gem,
So this, my first poem, is just for them!

Lily Stewart-Douglas (4)

Fun Frogs Day Nursery, Wilmslow

My First Poem

My name is **Amy** and I go to preschool,
My best friend is **Alana-Rose**, who is really cool.
I watch **Peppa Pig** on TV,
Playing **on my scooter** is lots of fun for me.
I just love **sausage and chips** to eat,
And sometimes **ice cream** for a treat.
Pink is a colour I like a lot,
My **penguin** is the best present I ever got.
My favourite person is **Jack, my brother**, who is a gem,
So this, my first poem, is just for them!

Amy Lake (3)
Fun Frogs Day Nursery, Wilmslow

My First Poem

My name is George and I go to preschool,
My best friend is Ashar, who is really cool.
I watch Topsy and Tim on TV,
Playing football is lots of fun for me.
I just love chips and nuggets to eat,
And sometimes sweets for a treat.
Blue is a colour I like a lot,
My car is the best present I ever got.
My favourite person is my mummy, who is a gem,
So this, my first poem, is just for them!

George Prideaux (3)

Fun Frogs Day Nursery, Wilmslow

My First Poem

My name is **Lilah** and I go to preschool,
My best friend is **Georgina**, who is really cool.
I watch **Go Jetters** on TV,
Playing **with the bricks** is lots of fun for me.
I just love **oranges and bananas** to eat,
And sometimes **chocolate** for a treat.
Pink is a colour I like a lot,
My **bike** is the best present I ever got.
My favourite person is **Mummy**, who is a gem,
So this, my first poem, is just for them!

Lilah Glasby (3)
Gershwin Park Day Nursery School, Witham

My First Poem

My name is **Jamie** and I go to preschool,
My best friend is **Katie**, who is really cool.
I watch **Big Hero 6** on TV,
Playing **football** is lots of fun for me.
I just love **fish fingers, chips, sauce and toast** to eat,
And sometimes **cake and biscuits** for a treat.
Red is a colour I like a lot,
My **sister** is the best present I ever got.
My favourite person is **Grandad Baldy Man**, who is a gem,
So this, my first poem, is just for them!

Jamie Jonathan Robert Buttress (3)

Gershwin Park Day Nursery School, Witham

My First Poem

My name is **Tyler** and I go to preschool,
My best friend is **Sienna**, who is really cool.
I watch **Jake and the Never Land Pirates** on TV,
Playing **hide-and-seek** is lots of fun for me.
I just love **chicken curry and rice or pizza and chips** to eat,
And sometimes **Fruit Pastilles** for a treat.
Blue is a colour I like a lot,
My **Leo sword** is the best present I ever got.
My favourite person is **my mummy**, who is a gem,
So this, my first poem, is just for them!

Tyler Hawthorne (3)
Gershwin Park Day Nursery School, Witham

My First Poem

My name is **Samuel** and I go to preschool,
My best friend is **Jessica**, who is really cool.
I watch **Jelly Jamm** on TV,
Playing **with trains** is lots of fun for me.
I just love **porridge and apples** to eat,
And sometimes **custard** for a treat.
Yellow is a colour I like a lot,
My **music CD** is the best present I ever got.
My favourite person is **Emily**, who is a gem,
So this, my first poem, is just for them!

Samuel Frederick Baxter (4)

Gershwin Park Day Nursery School, Witham

My First Poem

My name is Daan and I go to preschool,
My best friend is Samuel, who is really cool.
I watch planes on TV,
Playing with cars is lots of fun for me.
I just love pasta to eat,
And sometimes custard for a treat.
Blue is a colour I like a lot,
My train set is the best present I ever got.
My favourite person is Grandma, who is a gem,
So this, my first poem, is just for them!

Daan Verstraete (3)

Gershwin Park Day Nursery School, Witham

My First Poem

My name is **Noah** and I go to preschool,
My best friend is **Toby, my pet dog**, who is really cool.
I watch **PAW Patrol and Andy's Dinosaur Adventures** on TV,
Playing **with my big truck** is lots of fun for me.
I just love **dinner and breakfast** to eat,
And sometimes **Smarties** for a treat.
Blue is a colour I like a lot,
My **lorry** is the best present I ever got.
My favourite person is **Jo Jo**, who is a gem,
So this, my first poem, is just for them!

Noah Barker (3)

Gershwin Park Day Nursery School, Witham

My First Poem

My name is **Ava** and I go to preschool,
My best friend is **Mummy**, who is really cool.
I watch **Mickey Mouse Clubhouse** on TV,
Playing **tea parties** is lots of fun for me.
I just love **pears** to eat,
And sometimes **chocolate** for a treat.
Pink is a colour I like a lot,
My **doll's house** is the best present I ever got.
My favourite person is **Ruby**, who is a gem,
So this, my first poem, is just for them!

Ava Williams (3)

Gershwin Park Day Nursery School, Witham

My First Poem

My name is **Erin** and I go to preschool,
My best friend is **Connor**, who is really cool.
I watch **Bing** on TV,
Playing **with building blocks** is lots of fun for me.
I just love **sausages** to eat,
And sometimes **chocolate** for a treat.
Pink is a colour I like a lot,
My **kitchen** is the best present I ever got.
My favourite person is **Mummy**, who is a gem,
So this, my first poem, is just for them!

Erin Dymock (2)
Gershwin Park Day Nursery School, Witham

My First Poem

My name is **Chloe** and I go to preschool,
My best friends are **Abigail and Katie**, who are really cool.
I watch **Thomas the Tank Engine** on TV,
Playing **with Play-Doh** is lots of fun for me.
I just love **cheese** to eat,
And sometimes **Maltesers** for a treat.
Blue is a colour I like a lot,
My **horse stable** is the best present I ever got.
My favourite person is **Nanny**, who is a gem,
So this, my first poem, is just for them!

Chloe McColm (4)
Gershwin Park Day Nursery School, Witham

My First Poem

My name is **Katie** and I go to preschool,
My best friends are **Isabelle and Chloe**, who are really cool.
I watch **Thomas the Tank Engine** on TV,
Playing **hide-and-seek** is lots of fun for me.
I just love **olives and cheese** to eat,
And sometimes **Smarties** for a treat.
Pink is a colour I like a lot,
My **dinosaurs** are the best present I ever got.
My favourite person is **Nanny**, who is a gem,
So this, my first poem, is just for them!

Katie McColm (3)

Gershwin Park Day Nursery School, Witham

My First Poem

My name is **Milla** and I go to preschool,
My best friends are **Sethy, Isla, Kiki and Penny**, who are really cool.
I watch **Frozen** on TV,
Playing **hide-and-seek and fishing** is lots of fun for me.
I just love **an apple** to eat,
And sometimes **chocolate eggs with toys** for a treat.
Pink is a colour I like a lot,
My **princesses and my scooter** are the best presents I ever got.
My favourite people are **Mummy and Daddy**, who are gems,
So this, my first poem, is just for them!

Milla Elizabeth Ding (3)
Gershwin Park Day Nursery School, Witham

My First Poem

My name is Charlie and I go to preschool,
My best friend is Susannah, who is really cool.
I watch Peppa Pig on TV,
Playing with my toy robot is lots of fun for me.
I just love jam and honey sandwiches to eat,
And sometimes soup and bread for a treat.
Blue is a colour I like a lot,
My dolly is the best present I ever got.
My favourite person is Granny, who is a gem,
So this, my first poem, is just for them!

Charlie Dunmore (4)

Honeypot Day Nursery & Preschool, Spalding

My First Poem

My name is Wojciech and I go to preschool,
My best friend is Wiktoria, who is really cool.
I watch Thomas the Tank Engine on TV,
Playing with my trains is lots of fun for me.
I just love bananas to eat,
And sometimes chocolate for a treat.
Blue is a colour I like a lot,
My Thomas train is the best present I ever got.
My favourite person is Mummy, who is a gem,
So this, my first poem, is just for them!

Wojciech Jasnikowski (4)
Honeypot Day Nursery & Preschool, Spalding

My First Poem

My name is Dominic and I go to preschool,
My best friend is Wiktor, who is really cool.
I watch turtles on TV,
Playing robots is lots of fun for me.
I just love sandwiches to eat,
And sometimes chocolate for a treat.
Pink is a colour I like a lot,
My tractor is the best present I ever got.
My favourite person is Khloe, who is a gem,
So this, my first poem, is just for them!

Dominic Joshua Palmer (4)

Honeypot Day Nursery & Preschool, Spalding

My First Poem

My name is Florence and I go to preschool,
My best friend is Violet, who is really cool.
I watch CBeebies Bedtime on TV,
Playing with my Elsa and Anna dolls is lots of fun for me.
I just love sweetcorn, carrots and peas to eat,
And sometimes chocolate and crispies for a treat.
Pink is a colour I like a lot,
My Frozen pyjamas are the best present I ever got.
My favourite person is Mummy, who is a gem,
So this, my first poem, is just for them!

Florence Brown (3)
Honeypot Day Nursery & Preschool, Spalding

My First Poem

My name is Jaxon and I go to preschool,
My best friend is Connor, who is really cool.
I watch Fireman Sam on TV,
Playing Bob the Builder games is lots of fun for me.
I just love pizza to eat,
And sometimes sweeties for a treat.
Green is a colour I like a lot,
My Optimus Prime is the best present I ever got.
My favourite person is Daddy, who is a gem,
So this, my first poem, is just for them!

Jaxon Taplin (4)

Honeypot Day Nursery & Preschool, Spalding

My First Poem

My name is **Millie** and I go to preschool,
My best friend is **Ruby**, who is really cool.
I watch **PAW Patrol** on TV,
Playing **with my dolls** is lots of fun for me.
I just love **soup** to eat,
And sometimes **sweeties** for a treat.
Purple is a colour I like a lot,
My **dolly** is the best present I ever got.
My favourite person is **Daddy**, who is a gem,
So this, my first poem, is just for them!

Millie Rose Elderkin (4)

Honeypot Day Nursery & Preschool, Spalding

My First Poem

My name is **Susannah** and I go to preschool,
My best friend is **Violet**, who is really cool.
I watch **Bambi** on TV,
Playing **with my brother** is lots of fun for me.
I just love **pizza** to eat,
And sometimes **chocolate** for a treat.
Pink is a colour I like a lot,
My **Elsa and Anna dolls** are the best presents I ever got.
My favourite person is **Spencer**, who is a gem,
So this, my first poem, is just for them!

Susannah Poll (3)

Honeypot Day Nursery & Preschool, Spalding

My First Poem

My name is **Bonnie** and I go to preschool,
My best friend is **Skye**, who is really cool.
I watch **Peppa Pig** on TV,
Playing **with my Frozen dolls** is lots of fun for me.
I just love **Frozen bars** to eat,
And sometimes **a strawberry ice cream** for a treat.
Pink is a colour I like a lot,
My **Frozen toys** are the best presents I ever got.
My favourite person is **Mummy**, who is a gem,
So this, my first poem, is just for them!

Bonnie Beadle-Wright (3)
Honeypot Day Nursery & Preschool, Spalding

My First Poem

My name is **Abbi** and I go to preschool,
My best friend is **Morgan**, who is really cool.
I watch **Peppa Pig** on TV,
Playing **with my Rapunzel** is lots of fun for me.
I just love **nuggets and chips** to eat,
And sometimes **ice cream** for a treat.
Brown is a colour I like a lot,
My **Ariel** is the best present I ever got.
My favourite person is **Mummy**, who is a gem,
So this, my first poem, is just for them!

Abbi Johnson (3)

Honeypot Day Nursery & Preschool, Spalding

My First Poem

My name is **Ruby** and I go to preschool,
My best friend is **Alfie**, who is really cool.
I watch **Alvin and the Chipmunks** on TV,
Playing **with Poppy** is lots of fun for me.
I just love **sausages** to eat,
And sometimes **a milky chocolate bar** for a treat.
Pink is a colour I like a lot,
My **dinosaur** is the best present I ever got.
My favourite person is **Ellie**, who is a gem,
So this, my first poem, is just for them!

Ruby Mae Frith (3)
Honeypot Day Nursery & Preschool, Spalding

My First Poem

My name is **Tilley** and I go to preschool,
My best friend is **Alfie**, who is really cool.
I watch **Frozen** on TV,
Playing **with Elsa** is lots of fun for me.
I just love **sweetcorn** to eat,
And sometimes **fish fingers** for a treat.
Pink is a colour I like a lot,
My **computer** is the best present I ever got.
My favourite person is **Abbi**, who is a gem,
So this, my first poem, is just for them!

Matilda Motley-Webber (3)

Honeypot Day Nursery & Preschool, Spalding

My First Poem

My name is **Alfie** and I go to preschool,
My best friend is **Olly**, who is really cool.
I watch **Cinderella** on TV,
Playing **with my cars** is lots of fun for me.
I just love **mashed potato** to eat,
And sometimes **sweets** for a treat.
Black is a colour I like a lot,
My **Spider-Man** is the best present I ever got.
My favourite person is **Jo**, who is a gem,
So this, my first poem, is just for them!

Alfie Desmond (3)
Honeypot Day Nursery & Preschool, Spalding

My First Poem

My name is **Marley** and I go to preschool,
My best friend is **Brittany**, who is really cool.
I watch **Scooby-Doo** on TV,
Playing **with my blankies** is lots of fun for me.
I just love **Peperami** to eat,
And sometimes **yoghurt** for a treat.
Brown is a colour I like a lot,
My **paints** are the best present I ever got.
My favourite person is **Becky**, who is a gem,
So this, my first poem, is just for them!

Marley Bycraft (4)

Honeypot Day Nursery & Preschool, Spalding

My First Poem

My name is **Bianca** and I go to preschool,
My best friend is **my dad**, who is really cool.
I watch **Tom & Jerry** on TV,
Playing **Shopkins** is lots of fun for me.
I just love **cucumber** to eat,
And sometimes **chocolate** for a treat.
Pink is a colour I like a lot,
My **play donkey** is the best present I ever got.
My favourite person is **my aunty, Sarah**, who is a gem,
So this, my first poem, is just for them!

Bianca Cancela (3)
Joel Nursery, London

My First Poem

My name is **Tybias** and I go to preschool,
My best friend is **Tyella**, who is really cool.
I watch **PAW Patrol** on TV,
Playing **racing cars** is lots of fun for me.
I just love **vegetables** to eat,
And sometimes **chocolate cake** for a treat.
Pink is a colour I like a lot,
My **racing car** is the best present I ever got.
My favourite person is **Daddy**, who is a gem,
So this, my first poem, is just for them!

Tybias Sinclair (3)

Joel Nursery, London

My First Poem

My name is Kaila and I go to preschool,
My best friend is Arianna, who is really cool.
I watch CBeebies on TV,
Playing Palace Pets games are lots of fun for me.
I just love burgers to eat,
And sometimes chocolate for a treat.
Pink is a colour I like a lot,
My dinosaur is the best present I ever got.
My favourite person is Nanny, who is a gem,
So this, my first poem, is just for them!

Kaila-Marie Smith-Weekes (4)
Joel Nursery, London

My First Poem

My name is **Balma** and I go to preschool,
My best friend is **Jason**, who is really cool.
I watch **Nick Junior** on TV,
Playing **with toys in my bed** is lots of fun for me.
I just love **spaghetti Bolognese** to eat,
And sometimes **chocolate** for a treat.
Brown is a colour I like a lot,
My **kitty cat face** is the best present I ever got.
My favourite person is **Jason**, who is a gem,
So this, my first poem, is just for them!

Balma Mballta (3)

Joel Nursery, London

My First Poem

My name is Aiden and I go to preschool,
My best friend is my jinu nana, who is really cool.
I watch PAW Patrol and Peppa Pig on TV,
Playing with cars, trucks and bin trucks is lots of fun for me.
I just love rice and spaghetti to eat,
And sometimes Wotsits and ice cream for a treat.
Green and red are colours I like a lot,
My big bin truck is the best present I ever got.
My favourite person is my mummy, who is a gem,
So this, my first poem, is just for them!

Aiden Dean Patel (2)

Joel Nursery, London

My First Poem

My name is Aryan and I go to preschool,
My best friend is Kaleel, who is really cool.
I watch Spider-Man on TV,
Playing with blocks is lots of fun for me.
I just love jelly to eat,
And sometimes chocolate for a treat.
Blue is a colour I like a lot,
My bike is the best present I ever got.
My favourite person is Ash, who is a gem,
So this, my first poem, is just for them!

Aryan Patel (4)

Kenton Day Nursery, Harrow

My First Poem

My name is Rohan and I go to preschool,
My best friend is Milli, who is really cool.
I watch elephants on TV,
Playing with animals is lots of fun for me.
I just love noodles to eat,
And sometimes chocolate for a treat.
Green is a colour I like a lot,
My elephant is the best present I ever got.
My favourite person is Milli, who is a gem,
So this, my first poem, is just for them!

Rohan Shah (3)

Kenton Day Nursery, Harrow

My First Poem

My name is **Aaheli** and I go to preschool,
My best friend is **Milli**, who is really cool.
I watch **Dora** on TV,
Playing **with building blocks** is lots of fun for me.
I just love **chicken and rice** to eat,
And sometimes **fish** for a treat.
Pink is a colour I like a lot,
My **bike** is the best present I ever got.
My favourite person is **my mom**, who is a gem,
So this, my first poem, is just for them!

Aaheli Roy (3)
Kenton Day Nursery, Harrow

My First Poem

My name is **Mehar** and I go to preschool,
My best friend is **Riana**, who is really cool.
I watch **Peppa Pig** on TV,
Playing **in the home corner** is lots of fun for me.
I just love **cheese** to eat,
And sometimes **chocolate** for a treat.
Yellow is a colour I like a lot,
My **cat** is the best present I ever got.
My favourite person is **Daddy**, who is a gem,
So this, my first poem, is just for them!

Mehar Jain (3)
Kenton Day Nursery, Harrow

My First Poem

My name is **Riana** and I go to preschool,
My best friends are **Meher, Sienna, Milli and Erica**, who are really cool.
I watch **kids stories and rhymes** on TV,
Playing **Peppa Pig games and teddy and lamb games** is lots of fun for me.
I just love **yummy pasta** to eat,
And sometimes **chocolate and cakes** for a treat.
Pink and red are colours I like a lot,
My **pink scooter** is the best present I ever got.
My favourite people are **my mummy and daddy**, who are gems,
So this, my first poem, is just for them!

Riana Ragel (3)

Kenton Day Nursery, Harrow

My First Poem

My name is **Kanaya** and I go to preschool,
My best friend is **Krish**, who is really cool.
I watch **Thomas the Tank Engine** on TV,
Playing **with cars and trains** is lots of fun for me.
I just love **peas and rice** to eat,
And sometimes **ice cream** for a treat.
Orange and blue are colours I like a lot,
My **trains (Henry, James and Thomas)** are the best presents I ever got.
My favourite person is **my mummy**, who is a gem,
So this, my first poem, is just for them!

Kanaya Samani (3)
Kenton Day Nursery, Harrow

My First Poem

My name is **Madeleine** and I go to preschool,
My best friend is **Madison**, who is really cool.
I watch **Sofia the First** on TV,
Playing **dressing up** is lots of fun for me.
I just love **vegetable pasta** to eat,
And sometimes **chocolate** for a treat.
Pink is a colour I like a lot,
My **princess doll** is the best present I ever got.
My favourite person is **Daddy**, who is a gem,
So this, my first poem, is just for them!

Madeleine Floyd (3)
Ladybird Forest Preschool, Bedford

My First Poem

My name is **Lucas** and I go to preschool,
My best friend is **Dexter**, who is really cool.
I watch **Peppa Pig** on TV,
Playing **with building blocks** is lots of fun for me.
I just love **oranges and grapes** to eat,
And sometimes **choc choc** for a treat.
Green is a colour I like a lot,
My **bike** is the best present I ever got.
My favourite person is **Mummy**, who is a gem,
So this, my first poem, is just for them!

Lucas Hickman (3)
Ladybird Forest Preschool, Bedford

My First Poem

My name is Zoe and I go to preschool,
My best friend is Abby, who is really cool.
I watch Topsy and Tim on TV,
Playing with my doll's house is lots of fun for me.
I just love sausage and mash to eat,
And sometimes ice cream for a treat.
Yellow is a colour I like a lot,
My play tent is the best present I ever got.
My favourite person is Mummy, who is a gem,
So this, my first poem, is just for them!

Zoe Harding (4)
Ladybird Forest Preschool, Bedford

My First Poem

My name is **Scarlett** and I go to preschool,
My best friend is **Keida**, who is really cool.
I watch **Ben & Holly** on TV,
Playing **football** is lots of fun for me.
I just love **food** to eat,
And sometimes **sweets** for a treat.
Yellow is a colour I like a lot,
My **dolly** is the best present I ever got.
My favourite person is **Mummy**, who is a gem,
So this, my first poem, is just for them!

Scarlett Stocker (2)
Ladybird Forest Preschool, Bedford

My First Poem

My name is Dylan and I go to preschool,
My best friend is Jacob, who is really cool.
I watch PAW Patrol on TV,
Playing with trains is lots of fun for me.
I just love ice cream to eat,
And sometimes more ice cream for a treat.
Green is a colour I like a lot,
My PAW Patrol lunch bag is the best present I ever got.
My favourite person is Jacob, who is a gem,
So this, my first poem, is just for them!

Dylan Sylvester (3)
Ladybird Forest Preschool, Bedford

My First Poem

My name is **Evie** and I go to preschool,
My best friends are **May, Lottie, Rosie and Penny**, who are really cool.
I watch **Frozen** on TV,
Playing **schools** is lots of fun for me.
I just love **McDonald's** to eat,
And sometimes **sweeties** for a treat.
Yellow and blue are colours I like a lot,
My **Baby Annabell** is the best present I ever got.
My favourite person is **Mummy**, who is a gem,
So this, my first poem, is just for them!

Evie Isabella Sheridan (3)
Ladybird Forest Preschool, Bedford

My First Poem

My name is **Isabel** and I go to preschool,
My best friend is **Oliver**, who is really cool.
I watch **Topsy and Tim** on TV,
Playing **collecting treasures** is lots of fun for me.
I just love **mango** to eat,
And sometimes **chips** for a treat.
Purple is a colour I like a lot,
My **doll, Jenny,** is the best present I ever got.
My favourite person is **Grandma**, who is a gem,
So this, my first poem, is just for them!

Isabel Grace McCrindle (3)

Ladybird Forest Preschool, Bedford

My First Poem

My name is **Lavinia** and I go to preschool,
My best friend is **Jack**, who is really cool.
I watch **Peppa Pig** on TV,
Playing **Let It Go** is lots of fun for me.
I just love **chocolate, sweets and Milkybars** to eat,
And sometimes **hot chocolate jelly beans** for a treat.
Pink, purple and yellow are colours I like a lot,
My **Shopkins** are the best present I ever got.
My favourite person is **Kulfi, the dog**, who is a gem,
So this, my first poem, is just for them!

Lavinia Jean Waller (4)
Ladybird Forest Preschool, Bedford

My First Poem

My name is Jackson and I go to preschool,
My best friends are Jago and Jasper, who are really cool.
I watch Andy's Dinosaur Adventures on TV,
Playing little dinosaurs is lots of fun for me.
I just love a burger and plastic cheese to eat,
And sometimes an ice lolly for a treat.
Yellow, green and blue are colours I like a lot,
My iPad is the best present I ever got.
My favourite people are Jasper and Jago, who are gems,
So this, my first poem, is just for them!

Jackson Gray Amis (3)
Ladybird Forest Preschool, Bedford

My First Poem

My name is **Grace** and I go to preschool,
My best friends are **Rita, Amy and Joshua**, who are really cool.
I watch **Peppa Pig** on TV,
Playing **dress-up and shopping** is lots of fun for me.
I just love **pasta** to eat,
And sometimes **chocolate** for a treat.
Pink is a colour I like a lot,
My **Woody, Jessie and Buzz** are the best presents I ever got.
My favourite person is **Mummy**, who is a gem,
So this, my first poem, is just for them!

Grace Marabese (2)
Ladybird Forest Preschool, Bedford

My First Poem

My name is **Eliza** and I go to preschool,
My best friend is **Oliver**, who is really cool.
I watch **Peppa Pig** on TV,
Playing **with my dollies** is lots of fun for me.
I just love **sausages** to eat,
And sometimes **chocolate** for a treat.
Purple is a colour I like a lot,
My **Octonauts** are the best present I ever got.
My favourite person is **Grandad**, who is a gem,
So this, my first poem, is just for them!

Eliza Wilkinson (3)
Ladybird Forest Preschool, Bedford

My First Poem

My name is **Evie** and I go to preschool,
My best friends are **Etta and Freya**, who are really cool.
I watch **Minions** on TV,
Playing **with My Little Pony and Batman** is lots of fun for me.
I just love **cheese** to eat,
And sometimes **a chocolate egg** for a treat.
Blue is a colour I like a lot,
My **miaow cat** is the best present I ever got.
My favourite people are **Freya, Mummy and Daddy**, who are gems,
So this, my first poem, is just for them!

Evie Spencer (3)
Ladybird Forest Preschool, Bedford

My First Poem

My name is **Herbie** and I go to preschool,
My best friend is **Joshua**, who is really cool.
I watch **Horrid Henry** on TV,
Playing **on trains** is lots of fun for me.
I just love **beans and sausages** to eat,
And sometimes **sweets from the sweet shop** for a treat.
Blue is a colour I like a lot,
My **shop** is the best present I ever got.
My favourite person is **Daddy**, who is a gem,
So this, my first poem, is just for them!

Herbie Paterson (4)

Ladybird Forest Preschool, Bedford

My First Poem

My name is Larni and I go to preschool,
My best friends are Autumn, Ella, Rosie,
Lottie and Josh, who are really cool.
I watch Paddington Bear on TV,
Playing with the Barbie house is lots of fun
for me.
I just love chicken goujons to eat,
And sometimes chocolate Crunchies for
a treat.
Yellow is a colour I like a lot,
My Stretchkin is the best present I ever got.
My favourite person is Georgie, my cousin, who is
a gem,
So this, my first poem, is just for them!

Larni Rose Jones (4)
Ladybird Forest Preschool, Bedford

My First Poem

My name is **Jasper** and I go to preschool,
My best friend is **Jamie**, who is really cool.
I watch **Team Umizoomi** on TV,
Playing **superheroes** is lots of fun for me.
I just love **apples** to eat,
And sometimes **ice cream** for a treat.
Blue is a colour I like a lot,
My **Spider-Man** is the best present I ever got.
My favourite person is **Jonah**, who is a gem,
So this, my first poem, is just for them!

Jasper Doohan (4)
Ladybird Forest Preschool, Bedford

My First Poem

My name is **Joshua** and I go to preschool,
My best friend is **Imogen**, who is really cool.
I watch **PAW Patrol** on TV,
Playing **doctors and nurses** is lots of fun for me.
I just love **fish fingers** to eat,
And sometimes **ice cream** for a treat.
Pink is a colour I like a lot,
My **toy horse** is the best present I ever got.
My favourite person is **Daddy**, who is a gem,
So this, my first poem, is just for them!

Joshua Tomlinson

Little Acorns Nursery, Leicester

My First Poem

My name is **Vikram** and I go to preschool,
My best friend is **Harveer**, who is really cool.
I watch **Home Alone** on TV,
Playing **with toys** is lots of fun for me.
I just love **fish** to eat,
And sometimes **chocolate** for a treat.
Red is a colour I like a lot,
My **Hedgehog** is the best present I ever got.
My favourite person is **Harveer**, who is a gem,
So this, my first poem, is just for them!

Vikram Sahdev (3)

Little Acorns Nursery, Leicester

My First Poem

My name is **Dilraj** and I go to preschool,
My best friend is **Sebastian**, who is really cool.
I watch **Home Alone** on TV,
Playing **with cars** is lots of fun for me.
I just love **fish** to eat,
And sometimes **chocolate** for a treat.
Black is a colour I like a lot,
My **bow and arrow set** is the best present I ever got.
My favourite person is **Sebastian**, who is a gem,
So this, my first poem, is just for them!

Dilraj Sahdev (4)

Little Acorns Nursery, Leicester

My First Poem

My name is Diiya and I go to preschool,
My best friend is Maya, who is really cool.
I watch Ben & Holly on TV,
Playing with my doctor set is lots of fun for me.
I just love pizza to eat,
And sometimes chocolate buttons for a treat.
Red is a colour I like a lot,
My Peppa Pig is the best present I ever got.
My favourite person is Mummy, who is a gem,
So this, my first poem, is just for them!

Diiya Bharakhda (3)

Little Acorns Nursery, Leicester

My First Poem

My name is **Jasper** and I go to preschool,
My best friend is **Tiggy**, who is really cool.
I watch **PAW Patrol** on TV,
Playing **with cars** is lots of fun for me.
I just love **spaghetti** to eat,
And sometimes **chocolate** for a treat.
Yellow is a colour I like a lot,
My **Mike toy** is the best present I ever got.
My favourite person is **Tiggy**, who is a gem,
So this, my first poem, is just for them!

Jasper Jan Anderson (3)

Little Acorns Nursery, Leicester

My First Poem

My name is **Langelihle** and I go to preschool,
My best friend is **Mummy**, who is really cool.
I watch **racing cars** on TV,
Playing **with diggers** is lots of fun for me.
I just love **lollies** to eat,
And sometimes **sweets** for a treat.
Red is a colour I like a lot,
My **rocket** is the best present I ever got.
My favourite person is **Mummy**, who is a gem,
So this, my first poem, is just for them!

Langelihle Rishi Booi (2)

Little Acorns Nursery, Leicester

My First Poem

My name is **Amar** and I go to preschool,
My best friend is **Theo**, who is really cool.
I watch **The Lion Guard** on TV,
Playing **with my sister** Roop is lots of fun for me.
I just love **bananas** to eat,
And sometimes **yoghurt** for a treat.
Black is a colour I like a lot,
My **Lego space rocket** is the best present I ever got.
My favourite person is **Mummy**, who is a gem,
So this, my first poem, is just for them!

Amar Singh Ruprai (3)

Little Acorns Nursery, Leicester

My First Poem

My name is **Elisha** and I go to preschool,
My best friend is **Sebastian**, who is really cool.
I watch **Teletubbies** on TV,
Playing **with trains** is lots of fun for me.
I just love **cheesy pasta** to eat,
And sometimes **sweets** for a treat.
Pink is a colour I like a lot,
My **flower** is the best present I ever got.
My favourite person is **Poppy**, who is a gem,
So this, my first poem, is just for them!

Elisha Hope Alice Matu (4)

Little Acorns Nursery, Leicester

My First Poem

My name is Poppy and I go to preschool,
My best friend is Tiggy, who is really cool.
I watch PAW Patrol on TV,
Playing with Anna is lots of fun for me.
I just love pasta with cheese to eat,
And sometimes chocolate cake for a treat.
Purple is a colour I like a lot,
My Anna is the best present I ever got.
My favourite person is Violet, who is a gem,
So this, my first poem, is just for them!

Poppy Rhodes
Little Acorns Nursery, Leicester

My First Poem

My name is **Billy** and I go to preschool,
My best friend is **Tiana**, who is really cool.
I watch **Teletubbies** on TV,
Playing **with my blue car** is lots of fun for me.
I just love **toast** to eat,
And sometimes **chocolate cake** for a treat.
Black is a colour I like a lot,
My **Elsa** is the best present I ever got.
My favourite person is **Tiana**, who is a gem,
So this, my first poem, is just for them!

Billy Beau Brandreth (3)

Little Acorns Nursery, Leicester

My First Poem

My name is **Theo** and I go to preschool,
My best friend is **Billy**, who is really cool.
I watch **Mike the Knight** on TV,
Playing **Iron Man** is lots of fun for me.
I just love **chicken noodle soup** to eat,
And sometimes **cake** for a treat.
Green is a colour I like a lot,
My **Octonauts** are the best present I ever got.
My favourite person is **Amar**, who is a gem,
So this, my first poem, is just for them!

Theo Culverwell

Little Acorns Nursery, Leicester

My First Poem

My name is **Harveer** and I go to preschool,
My best friend is **Lily**, who is really cool.
I watch **Mr Tumble** on TV,
Playing **jigsaw puzzles** is lots of fun for me.
I just love **Weetabix** to eat,
And sometimes **sweets** for a treat.
Black is a colour I like a lot,
My **Duplo** is the best present I ever got.
My favourite person is **Billy**, who is a gem,
So this, my first poem, is just for them!

Harveer Singh Loyal (3)

Little Acorns Nursery, Leicester

My First Poem

My name is **Leonard** and I go to preschool,
My best friend is **Harveer**, who is really cool.
I watch **In the Night Garden** on TV,
Playing **Igglepiggle** is lots of fun for me.
I just love **pasta** to eat,
And sometimes **chocolate** for a treat.
Red is a colour I like a lot,
My **Rudolph** is the best present I ever got.
My favourite people are **Mummy and Daddy**, who are gems,
So this, my first poem, is just for them!

Leonard John Trevelyan Miller (2)

Little Acorns Nursery, Leicester

My First Poem

My name is **Reuben** and I go to preschool,
My best friend is **Albie**, who is really cool.
I watch **Toy Story** on TV,
Playing **Pokémon games** is lots of fun for me.
I just love **pasta** to eat,
And sometimes **chocolate coins** for a treat.
Grey is a colour I like a lot,
My **dinosaur eggs** are the best present I ever got.
My favourite person is **Granny**, who is a gem,
So this, my first poem, is just for them!

Reuben Louis Hampson-Goodyear (3)
Little Acorns Nursery, Leicester

My First Poem

My name is **Imogen** and I go to preschool,
My best friend is **Josh**, who is really cool.
I watch **Blaze** on TV,
Playing **with My Little Pony** is lots of fun for me.
I just love **gammon** to eat,
And sometimes **Kinder eggs** for a treat.
Orange is a colour I like a lot,
My **My Little Pony stage** is the best present I ever got.
My favourite person is **Mummy**, who is a gem,
So this, my first poem, is just for them!

Imogen Fearne Burrows (3)
Little Acorns Nursery, Leicester

My First Poem

My name is Samantha and I go to preschool,
My best friends are Maya and Ruby, who are really cool.
I watch Cinderella on TV,
Playing with my make-up is lots of fun for me.
I just love spaghetti hoops to eat,
And sometimes custard for a treat.
Pink is a colour I like a lot,
My princess doll is the best present I ever got.
My favourite person is Mummy, who is a gem,
So this, my first poem, is just for them!

Samantha Grace De Villiers (4)

Little Cherubs Day Nursery, Bromley

My First Poem

My name is **Malaika** and I go to preschool,
My best friend is **Gezal**, who is really cool.
I watch **Frozen** on TV,
Playing **with my babies and pushchair** is lots of fun for me.
I just love **spaghetti** to eat,
And sometimes **ice cream** for a treat.
White is a colour I like a lot,
My **fish tank with fishes** is the best present I ever got.
My favourite person is **Mummy**, who is a gem,
So this, my first poem, is just for them!

Malaika Khoso (2)
Little Cherubs Day Nursery, Bromley

My First Poem

My name is **Gezal** and I go to preschool,
My best friend is **Chanel**, who is really cool.
I watch **Peppa Pig** on TV,
Playing **with babies** is lots of fun for me.
I just love **spaghetti** to eat,
And sometimes **cake** for a treat.
Red is a colour I like a lot,
My **teddy** is the best present I ever got.
My favourite person is **Mummy**, who is a gem,
So this, my first poem, is just for them!

Gezal Mehdipour (3)

Little Cherubs Day Nursery, Bromley

My First Poem

My name is Grace and I go to preschool,
My best friend is Lily, who is really cool.
I watch Peppa Pig on TV,
Playing with the doll's house is lots of fun for me.
I just love sausages to eat,
And sometimes lemon cake in the café for a treat.
Pink is a colour I like a lot,
My Christmas book is the best present I ever got.
My favourite person is Mummy, who is a gem,
So this, my first poem, is just for them!

Grace Garatti-Lloyd (3)
Little Cherubs Day Nursery, Bromley

My First Poem

My name is **Lacey** and I go to preschool,
My best friend is **Evie**, who is really cool.
I watch **Frozen** on TV,
Playing **with the dressing-up clothes** is lots of fun for me.
I just love **broccoli and strawberries** to eat,
And sometimes **ice cream** for a treat.
Red is a colour I like a lot,
My **doll** is the best present I ever got.
My favourite person is **Mickie, my brother**, who is a gem,
So this, my first poem, is just for them!

Lacey-Jayne Ellis (3)
Little Cherubs Day Nursery, Bromley

My First Poem

My name is **Abbie** and I go to preschool,
My best friend is **Connor**, who is really cool.
I watch **Peppa Pig** on TV,
Playing **with my dollies** is lots of fun for me.
I just love **pizza** to eat,
And sometimes **ice cream** for a treat.
Red is a colour I like a lot,
My **Frozen Fever Elsa dress** is the best present I ever got.
My favourite person is **Mummy**, who is a gem,
So this, my first poem, is just for them!

Abbie Wood (3)
Little Cherubs Day Nursery, Bromley

My First Poem

My name is **Leo** and I go to preschool,
My best friend is **Oliver**, who is really cool.
I watch **Go Jetters** on TV,
Playing **with my train set** is lots of fun for me.
I just love **hot dogs and sushi** to eat,
And sometimes **rice cakes** for a treat.
Green is a colour I like a lot,
My **bumper car** is the best present I ever got.
My favourite person is **my brother,
Jonathan,** who is a gem,
So this, my first poem, is just for them!

Leo Harriss (3)

Little Cherubs Day Nursery, Bromley

My First Poem

My name is **Ruby** and I go to preschool,
My best friend is **Emily**, who is really cool.
I watch **Rapunzel** on TV,
Playing **with Lego** is lots of fun for me.
I just love **pasta and cheese** to eat,
And sometimes **cake and custard** for a treat.
Purple is a colour I like a lot,
My **doggy teddy** is the best present I ever got.
My favourite people are **Mummy and Daddy**, who are gems,
So this, my first poem, is just for them!

Ruby Slatter (3)
Little Cherubs Day Nursery, Bromley

My First Poem

My name is **Elisa** and I go to preschool,
My best friend is **Elliott**, who is really cool.
I watch **Peppa Pig** on TV,
Playing **with my doll's house** is lots of fun for me.
I just love **noodles** to eat,
And sometimes **ice cream** for a treat.
Blue is a colour I like a lot,
My **dolly** is the best present I ever got.
My favourite person is **Mummy**, who is a gem,
So this, my first poem, is just for them!

Elisa Wong (4)
Little Cherubs Day Nursery, Bromley

My First Poem

My name is **Maxwell** and I go to preschool,
My best friend is **Max**, who is really cool.
I watch **Thomas the Tank Engine** on TV,
Playing **with jumbo jets** is lots of fun for me.
I just love **sausages and chips** to eat,
And sometimes **cake and custard** for a treat.
Red is a colour I like a lot,
My **dragon drop** is the best present I ever got.
My favourite person is **Mummy**, who is a gem,
So this, my first poem, is just for them!

Maxwell Hawker (4)

Little Cherubs Day Nursery, Bromley

My First Poem

My name is Charlie and I go to preschool,
My best friend is Alexander, who is really cool.
I watch Toy Story on TV,
Playing with cars is lots of fun for me.
I just love pasta to eat,
And sometimes ice cream for a treat.
White is a colour I like a lot,
My flashing Lightning McQueen is the best present I ever got.
My favourite person is Mummy, who is a gem,
So this, my first poem, is just for them!

Charlie Parker (4)

Little Cherubs Day Nursery, Bromley

My First Poem

My name is **Andrea** and I go to preschool,
My best friends are **Mia and Khaleesi**, who are really cool.
I watch **Bogyó és Babóca** on TV,
Playing **the crocodile game** is lots of fun for me.
I just love **pasta** to eat,
And sometimes **chocolate** for a treat.
Pink is a colour I like a lot,
My **Baby Born** is the best present I ever got.
My favourite people are **Jess and Chloe**, who are gems,
So this, my first poem, is just for them!

Andrea Reischig (2)
Little Explorers Day Nursery, Leicester

My First Poem

My name is Mia Bella and I go to preschool,
My best friends are Andy, Khaleesi and Sasha, who are really cool.
I watch films and programmes on TV,
Playing Where's My Cupcake? is lots of fun for me.
I just love chicken, rice and vegetables to eat,
And sometimes sweets in a bowl for a treat.
Red is a colour I like a lot,
My Hungry Hippos game is the best present I ever got.
My favourite people are Daddy, Mummy, Fluffy, Bubbles and Sweetpea, who are gems,
So this, my first poem, is just for them!

Mia Bella Puna (3)

Little Explorers Day Nursery, Leicester

My First Poem

My name is Khaleesi and I go to preschool,
My best friends are everyone, who are really cool.
I watch Peppa Pig and Goldie & Bear on TV,
Playing games with my friends is lots of fun for me.
I just love baking cakes to eat,
And sometimes giving them to my friends for a treat.
Yellow is a colour I like a lot,
My Frozen watch is the best present I ever got.
My favourite person is Mummy, who is a gem,
So this, my first poem, is just for them!

Khaleesi Allsop (2)
Little Explorers Day Nursery, Leicester

My First Poem

My name is **Kayleigh** and I go to preschool,
My best friends are **Thomas and Isabell**, who are really cool.
I watch **Frozen** on TV,
Playing **games with my sister** is lots of fun for me.
I just love **pancakes** to eat,
And sometimes **ice cream** for a treat.
Pink and purple are colours I like a lot,
My **car game** is the best present I ever got.
My favourite person is **my mum**, who is a gem,
So this, my first poem, is just for them!

Kayleigh Campbell (3)
Little Explorers Day Nursery, Leicester

My First Poem

My name is Arlo and I go to preschool,
My best friend is Elisha, who is really cool.
I watch Star Wars on TV,
Playing superheroes is lots of fun for me.
I just love bananas to eat,
And sometimes ice cream for a treat.
Blue is a colour I like a lot,
My Batman BatBot is the best present I ever got.
My favourite person is Ravi, who is a gem,
So this, my first poem, is just for them!

Arlo Zachary Jallands (4)
Little Explorers Day Nursery, Leicester

My First Poem

My name is **Will** and I go to preschool,
My best friend is **Taylor**, who is really cool.
I watch **Big Hero 6** on TV,
Playing **football** is lots of fun for me.
I just love **sausages** to eat,
And sometimes **chocolate** for a treat.
Pink is a colour I like a lot,
My **train set** is the best present I ever got.
My favourite people are **Mummy, Daddy and Grandma**, who are gems,
So this, my first poem, is just for them!

William Neilson (3)

Little Explorers Day Nursery, Leicester

My First Poem

My name is **Sasha** and I go to preschool,
My best friends are **Mia, Khaleesi and Andrea**, who are really cool.
I watch **Masha and the Bear** on TV,
Playing **with Daddy and Play-Doh** is lots of fun for me.
I just love **potatoes** to eat,
And sometimes **ice cream** for a treat.
Green is a colour I like a lot,
My **Medo, my teddy,** is the best present I ever got.
My favourite person is **teacher, Claire**, who is a gem,
So this, my first poem, is just for them!

Sasha Needham (2)
Little Explorers Day Nursery, Leicester

My First Poem

My name is Lucie and I go to preschool,
My best friend is Emma, who is really cool.
I watch Umizoomi on TV,
Playing Lego is lots of fun for me.
I just love cheese to eat,
And sometimes biscuits for a treat.
Pink is a colour I like a lot,
My clown is the best present I ever got.
My favourite person is Mummy, who is a gem,
So this, my first poem, is just for them!

Lucie Ada Edme-Brenot (4)

Patacake Day Nursery, Cambridge

My First Poem

My name is Ari and I go to preschool,
My best friend is Mennah, who is really cool.
I watch Peppa Pig on TV,
Playing houses is lots of fun for me.
I just love chocolate to eat,
And sometimes M&Ms for a treat.
Red is a colour I like a lot,
My iPad is the best present I ever got.
My favourite person is Lucie, who is a gem,
So this, my first poem, is just for them!

Ari Smith Posner (4)

Patacake Day Nursery, Cambridge

My First Poem

My name is Purdy and I go to preschool,
My best friends are Ynaelle, Sofia, Maya and Isobel, who are really cool.
I watch The Barbie Diaries on TV,
Playing teachers with my Barbies is lots of fun for me.
I just love pasta, olives and cheese to eat,
And sometimes chocolate bunnies for a treat.
Pink is a colour I like a lot,
My Cinderella dress and my talking kitty are the best presents I ever got.
My favourite person is Farah, who is a gem,
So this, my first poem, is just for them!

Prudence Millie Mallindine (4)

Red Balloon Day Nursery, Cobham

My First Poem

My name is **Elwood** and I go to preschool,
My best friend is **Nicholas**, who is really cool.
I watch **Minions** on TV,
Playing **Star Wars** is lots of fun for me.
I just love **pesto pasta** to eat,
And sometimes **crisps** for a treat.
Light blue is a colour I like a lot,
My **Snake Hot Wheels** is the best present I ever got.
My favourite person is **Alex**, who is a gem,
So this, my first poem, is just for them!

Elwood Tiernan (4)

Red Balloon Day Nursery, Cobham

My First Poem

My name is **Evie Willow Cook** and I go to preschool,
My best friend is **Hendrix**, who is really cool.
I watch **Frozen and Peppa Pig** on TV,
Playing **balancing** is lots of fun for me.
I just love **octopus and chicken** to eat,
And sometimes **chocolate** for a treat.
Purple and pink are colours I like a lot,
My **scooter** is the best present I ever got.
My favourite people are **Mummy and Daddy**, who are gems,
So this, my first poem, is just for them!

Evie Willow Cook

Red Balloon Day Nursery, Cobham

My First Poem

My name is Liya and I go to preschool,
My best friend is Holly, who is really cool.
I watch Peter Rabbit and Bing Bunny on TV,
Playing my Wii, Hungry Hippos and Kerplunk is lots of fun for me.
I just love pasta and cheese to eat,
And sometimes chocolate cupcakes and ice cream for a treat.
Pink and purple are colours I like a lot,
My bicycle with ribbons and a basket is the best present I ever got.
My favourite person is my daddy, Kashif, who is a gem,
So this, my first poem, is just for them!

Liya Shuja
Red Balloon Day Nursery, Cobham

My First Poem

My name is **Alice** and I go to preschool,
My best friend is **Olivia**, who is really cool.
I watch **Masha and the Bear** on TV,
Playing **princesses** is lots of fun for me.
I just love **sausage and pasta** to eat,
And sometimes **candy** for a treat.
Pink is a colour I like a lot,
My **Elsa dress** is the best present I ever got.
My favourite person is **Alan (teddy)**, who is a gem,
So this, my first poem, is just for them!

Alice Florence Berry (3)

Red Balloon Day Nursery, Cobham

My First Poem

My name is Holly and I go to preschool,
My best friend is Sinead, who is really cool.
I watch Hey Duggee and Peppa Pig on TV,
Playing with my teddies and my Barbies is lots of fun for me.
I just love pasta and broccoli to eat,
And sometimes flapjack and bread sticks for a treat.
Yellow is a colour I like a lot,
My helicopter is the best present I ever got.
My favourite person is Lola, who is a gem,
So this, my first poem, is just for them!

Holly Price (3)

Red Balloon Day Nursery, Cobham

My First Poem

My name is **Benjamin** and I go to preschool,
My best friend is **Aaron**, who is really cool.
I watch **PAW Patrol** on TV,
Playing **with my PAW Patrol toys** is lots of fun for me.
I just love **broccoli and spaghetti** to eat,
And sometimes **sweets** for a treat.
Red and blue are colours I like a lot,
My **digger** is the best present I ever got.
My favourite person is **Mummy**, who is a gem,
So this, my first poem, is just for them!

Benjamin Cobden (3)

Red Balloon Day Nursery, Cobham

My First Poem

My name is **Aaron** and I go to preschool,
My best friend is **Ben**, who is really cool.
I watch **Thomas and his Friends** on TV,
Playing **Mobilo with Ben** is lots of fun for me.
I just love **peanut butter sandwiches** to eat,
And sometimes **cake** for a treat.
Blue is a colour I like a lot,
My **Tidmouth Sheds track** is the best present I ever got.
My favourite person is **Daniel**, who is a gem,
So this, my first poem, is just for them!

Aaron Beardmore (3)
Red Balloon Day Nursery, Cobham

My First Poem

My name is Ischia and I go to preschool,
My best friend is Ava, who is really cool.
I watch Angelina Ballerina on TV,
Playing mummies and daddies is lots of fun for me.
I just love roast lunch to eat,
And sometimes chocolate cake for a treat.
Dark pink is a colour I like a lot,
My dark pink bicycle is the best present I ever got.
My favourite person is Nat Nat, who is a gem,
So this, my first poem, is just for them!

Ischia Heathfield (4)

Red Balloon Day Nursery, Cobham

My First Poem

My name is **Amber** and I go to preschool,
My best friend is **Cherrish**, who is really cool.
I watch **dinosaurs** on TV,
Playing **dollies** is lots of fun for me.
I just love **chips** to eat,
And sometimes **sweeties** for a treat.
Pink is a colour I like a lot,
My **dollies** are the best present I ever got.
My favourite person is **Ralphie, my brother**,
who is a gem,
So this, my first poem, is just for them!

Amber Šutka (4)

Roberts Day Nursery, Portsmouth

My First Poem

My name is **McKenzie** and I go to preschool,
My best friend is **Leo**, who is really cool.
I watch **Thomas the Train** on TV,
Playing **PAW Patrol** is lots of fun for me.
I just love **pizza** to eat,
And sometimes **cheeseburger** for a treat.
Red is a colour I like a lot,
My **train track** is the best present I ever got.
My favourite person is **Caroline**, who is a gem,
So this, my first poem, is just for them!

McKenzie Hudson (4)

Roberts Day Nursery, Portsmouth

My First Poem

My name is Cobie and I go to preschool,
My best friends are Mia and Mummy, who are really cool.
I watch PAW Patrol on TV,
Playing with my doll's house is lots of fun for me.
I just love cheese to eat,
And sometimes strawberries for a treat.
Pink is a colour I like a lot,
My yoghurt is the best present I ever got.
My favourite person is Mia, my sister, who is a gem,
So this, my first poem, is just for them!

Cobie Marshall (3)
Roberts Day Nursery, Portsmouth

My First Poem

My name is **Abigail** and I go to preschool,
My best friend is **Jade**, who is really cool.
I watch **Peppa Pig** on TV,
Playing **with Jade** is lots of fun for me.
I just love **spaghetti** to eat,
And sometimes **Peppa Pig cake** for a treat.
Pink is a colour I like a lot,
My **Peppa Pig kitchen** is the best present I ever got.
My favourite person is **Mummy**, who is a gem,
So this, my first poem, is just for them!

Abigail Walton (3)

Roberts Day Nursery, Portsmouth

My First Poem

My name is Essie and I go to preschool,
My best friend is Elsa, who is really cool.
I watch CBeebies on TV,
Playing with my toys is lots of fun for me.
I just love everything to eat,
And sometimes cake for a treat.
Pink is a colour I like a lot,
My new bike is the best present I ever got.
My favourite person is Olaf, who is a gem,
So this, my first poem, is just for them!

Esmee Mitchell-Farmer (2)
Roberts Day Nursery, Portsmouth

My First Poem

My name is **Charlie** and I go to preschool,
My best friend is **Tiegan**, who is really cool.
I watch **Peppa Pig** on TV,
Playing **with my brother** is lots of fun for me.
I just love **pizza** to eat,
And sometimes **sweeties** for a treat.
Blue is a colour I like a lot,
My **scooter** is the best present I ever got.
My favourite person is **Tiegan**, who is a gem,
So this, my first poem, is just for them!

Charlie Spratt (3)
Roberts Day Nursery, Portsmouth

My First Poem

My name is **Cherrish** and I go to preschool,
My best friend is **Timmy**, who is really cool.
I watch **Charlie and Lola** on TV,
Playing **with my toys in my bedroom** is lots of fun for me.
I just love **rolls** to eat,
And sometimes **pasta** for a treat.
Purple is a colour I like a lot,
My **blue bike** is the best present I ever got.
My favourite person is **my mum**, who is a gem,
So this, my first poem, is just for them!

Cherrish Clarke (4)
Roberts Day Nursery, Portsmouth

My First Poem

My name is **Bernard** and I go to preschool,
My best friend is **Mummy**, who is really cool.
I watch **Thomas** on TV,
Playing **drawing** is lots of fun for me.
I just love **pork** to eat,
And sometimes **cake, chocolate and biscuits** for a treat.
Yellow is a colour I like a lot,
My **Mummy's new baby** is the best present I ever got.
My favourite person is **Mummy**, who is a gem,
So this, my first poem, is just for them!

Ben Mendy (3)

Roberts Day Nursery, Portsmouth

My First Poem

My name is India and I go to preschool,
My best friend is Abi, who is really cool.
I watch Frozen on TV,
Playing house and going to Daddy's work is lots of fun for me.
I just love sandwiches to eat,
And sometimes KFC and McDonald's for a treat.
Red is a colour I like a lot,
My big Wendy house from Grandad is the best present I ever got.
My favourite people are Mum and Daddy, who are gems,
So this, my first poem, is just for them!

India Lewis-Connock (4)
Roberts Day Nursery, Portsmouth

My First Poem

My name is **Amara** and I go to preschool,
My best friend is **Abi**, who is really cool.
I watch **Frozen** on TV,
Playing **with Abi** is lots of fun for me.
I just love **anything that Mummy makes** to eat,
And sometimes **crackers** for a treat.
Pink is a colour I like a lot,
My **drawing** is the best present I ever got.
My favourite person is **Jade**, who is a gem,
So this, my first poem, is just for them!

Amara Egwuatu (3)
Roberts Day Nursery, Portsmouth

My First Poem

My name is **Logun** and I go to preschool,
My best friend is **Rihanna**, who is really cool.
I watch **Scooby-Doo** on TV,
Playing **on my Xbox** is lots of fun for me.
I just love **pizza** to eat,
And sometimes **toys** for a treat.
Blue is a colour I like a lot,
My **star monster** is the best present I ever got.
My favourite person is **Mummy**, who is a gem,
So this, my first poem, is just for them!

Logun Elston (4)
Roberts Day Nursery, Portsmouth

My First Poem

My name is **Freddie** and I go to preschool,
My best friend is **Leo**, who is really cool.
I watch **painting** on TV,
Playing **cars** is lots of fun for me.
I just love **ice cream** to eat,
And sometimes **chocolate** for a treat.
Blue and red are colours I like a lot,
My **belt** is the best present I ever got.
My favourite person is **Mummy**, who is a gem,
So this, my first poem, is just for them!

Freddie Harvey (3)

Roberts Day Nursery, Portsmouth

My First Poem

My name is **Emily** and I go to preschool,
My best friend is **Michaela**, who is really cool.
I watch **Peppa Pig** on TV,
Playing **dollies** is lots of fun for me.
I just love **carrots** to eat,
And sometimes **jelly** for a treat.
Blue is a colour I like a lot,
My **pig** is the best present I ever got.
My favourite person is **Mummy**, who is a gem,
So this, my first poem, is just for them!

Emily Coles (3)
Roberts Day Nursery, Portsmouth

My First Poem

My name is **Lilly Summer** and I go to preschool,
My best friend is **Ocean**, who is really cool.
I watch **Boomerang** on TV,
Playing **cooking dinner** is lots of fun for me.
I just love **pizza** to eat,
And sometimes **a chocolate egg** for a treat.
Red is a colour I like a lot,
My **Minnie Mouse scooter** is the best present I ever got.
My favourite person is **Ocean**, who is a gem,
So this, my first poem, Is just for them!

Lily Summer Ruddy (3)

Roberts Day Nursery, Portsmouth

My First Poem

My name is **Melah** and I go to preschool,
My best friend is **Lucja**, who is really cool.
I watch **princesses** on TV,
Playing **with Peppa Pig** is lots of fun for me.
I just love **spaghetti** to eat,
And sometimes **cake** for a treat.
Pink is a colour I like a lot,
My **Tinker Bell** is the best present I ever got.
My favourite person is **my mummy**, who is a gem,
So this, my first poem, is just for them!

Melah Bah (3)
Roberts Day Nursery, Portsmouth

My First Poem

My name is **Lucja** and I go to preschool,
My best friend is **my sister, Camilla**, who is really cool.
I watch **EastEnders** on TV,
Playing **and reading books** is lots of fun for me.
I just love **chocolate** to eat,
And sometimes **more chocolate** for a treat.
Pink is a colour I like a lot,
My **Rapunzel and Ariel** are the best presents I ever got.
My favourite person is **my mummy**, who is a gem,
So this, my first poem, is just for them!

Lucja Pioro (3)
Roberts Day Nursery, Portsmouth

My First Poem

My name is **Sade-Nia** and I go to preschool,
My best friend is **Maggie**, who is really cool.
I watch **Mr Tumble** on TV,
Playing **Barbies** is lots of fun for me.
I just love **pasta** to eat,
And sometimes **a chocolate bar** for a treat.
Pink is a colour I like a lot,
My **Frozen bag** is the best present I ever got.
My favourite person is **Daddy**, who is a gem,
So this, my first poem, is just for them!

Sade-Nia Tull (4)

Roberts Day Nursery, Portsmouth

My First Poem

My name is **Billy** and I go to preschool,
My best friend is **Cherrish**, who is really cool.
I watch **PAW Patrol** on TV,
Playing **on the computer** is lots of fun for me.
I just love **a snack** to eat,
And sometimes **sweets in a box** for a treat.
Blue is a colour I like a lot,
My **PAW Patrol house** is the best present I ever got.
My favourite person is **Cherrish**, who is a gem,
So this, my first poem, is just for them!

Billy Burgess (3)
Roberts Day Nursery, Portsmouth

My First Poem

My name is **Tiegan** and I go to preschool,
My best friend is **Charlie**, who is really cool.
I watch **Peppa Pig** on TV,
Playing **with Charlie** is lots of fun for me.
I just love **pizza** to eat,
And sometimes **a chocolate egg** for a treat.
Orange, yellow and green are colours I like a lot,
My **Minnie Mouse bike** is the best present I ever got.
My favourite person is **Darcy**, who is a gem,
So this, my first poem, is just for them!

Tiegan Dobson (3)
Roberts Day Nursery, Portsmouth

My First Poem

My name is **Maggie** and I go to preschool,
My best friend is **Sade-Nia**, who is really cool.
I watch **Peppa Pig** on TV,
Playing **Elsa** is lots of fun for me.
I just love **sweets** to eat,
And sometimes **strawberries** for a treat.
Pink is a colour I like a lot,
My **Elsa** is the best present I ever got.
My favourite person is **Mummy**, who is a gem,
So this, my first poem, is just for them!

Maggie May Stewart (3)
Roberts Day Nursery, Portsmouth

My First Poem

My name is Ocean-Lea and I go to preschool,
My best friend is Lily, who is really cool.
I watch Frozen on TV,
Playing cooking is lots of fun for me.
I just love pizza to eat,
And sometimes crispies for a treat.
Pink is a colour I like a lot,
My big yellow bag is the best present I ever got.
My favourite person is Daddy, who is a gem,
So this, my first poem, is just for them!

Ocean-Lea Morey (4)
Roberts Day Nursery, Portsmouth

My First Poem

My name is Evie and I go to preschool,
My best friend is Lexie, who is really cool.
I watch Fresh Beat Band of Spies on TV,
Playing outside is lots of fun for me.
I just love macaroni cheese to eat,
And sometimes chocolate for a treat.
Red is a colour I like a lot,
My Frozen jewellery box is the best present I ever got.
My favourite person is Mummy, who is a gem,
So this, my first poem, is just for them!

Evie Grace Hayes (4)

School House Nursery, Sandwich

My First Poem

My name is **Skye** and I go to preschool,
My best friends are **Lexi, Evie and Lyla**, who are really cool.
I watch **Teletubbies, Ben & Holly and Thomas** on TV,
Playing **puzzles** is lots of fun for me.
I just love **cheesey pasta** to eat,
And sometimes **Dad's chocolate** for a treat.
Pink is a colour I like a lot,
My **Ben & Holly cards** are the best present I ever got.
My favourite person is **Nanny Jane**, who is a gem,
So this, my first poem, is just for them!

Skye Gibbons (3)
School House Nursery, Sandwich

My First Poem

My name is **Poppy** and I go to preschool,
My best friend is **Callum**, who is really cool.
I watch **Peppa Pig** on TV,
Playing **Shopkins** is lots of fun for me.
I just love **pizza** to eat,
And sometimes **cake** for a treat.
Red is a colour I like a lot,
My **bike** is the best present I ever got.
My favourite person is **Daddy**, who is a gem,
So this, my first poem, is just for them!

Katie James (4)

Stepping Stones Private Day Nursery, Pershore

My First Poem

My name is **Callum** and I go to preschool,
My best friend is **Elise**, who is really cool.
I watch **Ben & Holly** on TV,
Playing **cars** is lots of fun for me.
I just love **cabbage** to eat,
And sometimes **sweets** for a treat.
Pink is a colour I like a lot,
My **Thomas train** is the best present I ever got.
My favourite person is **Jacob**, who is a gem,
So this, my first poem, is just for them!

Callum Webb (3)
Stepping Stones Private Day Nursery, Pershore

My First Poem

My name is Morgan and I go to preschool,
My best friend is James, who is really cool.
I watch Balamory on TV,
Playing Duplo is lots of fun for me.
I just love wraps to eat,
And sometimes ice cream for a treat.
Purple is a colour I like a lot,
My Duplo is the best present I ever got.
My favourite person is Tasmin, who is a gem,
So this, my first poem, is just for them!

Morgan Archer-Smith (3)

Stepping Stones Private Day Nursery, Pershore

My First Poem

My name is **Maddison** and I go to preschool,
My best friend is **Alfie**, who is really cool.
I watch **Peppa Pig** on TV,
Playing **teddies** is lots of fun for me.
I just love **grapes** to eat,
And sometimes **chocolate** for a treat.
Pink is a colour I like a lot,
My **bike** is the best present I ever got.
My favourite person is **Maximus**, who is a gem,
So this, my first poem, is just for them!

Maddison Young (3)

Stepping Stones Private Day Nursery, Pershore

My First Poem

My name is Edward and I go to preschool,
My best friend is Max, who is really cool.
I watch Disney Cars on TV,
Playing cars is lots of fun for me.
I just love potatoes to eat,
And sometimes sweets for a treat.
Yellow is a colour I like a lot,
My cars are the best present I ever got.
My favourite person is Mummy, who is a gem,
So this, my first poem, is just for them!

Edward George Dorrell (3)

Stepping Stones Private Day Nursery, Pershore

My First Poem

My name is **Nicole** and I go to preschool,
My best friend is **Olivia**, who is really cool.
I watch **Peppa Pig** on TV,
Playing **outside** is lots of fun for me.
I just love **pasta** to eat,
And sometimes **chocolate** for a treat.
Green is a colour I like a lot,
My **basketball** is the best present I ever got.
My favourite person is **Mummy**, who is a gem,
So this, my first poem, is just for them!

Nicole Amelia Price (2)
Stepping Stones Private Day Nursery, Pershore

My First Poem

My name is **Paula** and I go to preschool,
My best friend is **Amelia**, who is really cool.
I watch **My Little Pony** on TV,
Playing **with dolls** is lots of fun for me.
I just love **pasta** to eat,
And sometimes **chocolate** for a treat.
Pink is a colour I like a lot,
My **baby doll** is the best present I ever got.
My favourite person is **Sara**, who is a gem,
So this, my first poem, is just for them!

Paula Gomez (3)

Teddies Southampton, Southampton

My First Poem

My name is **Samuel** and I go to preschool,
My best friend is **Riley**, who is really cool.
I watch **Spider-Man** on TV,
Playing **Batman** is lots of fun for me.
I just love **toast** to eat,
And sometimes **chocolate** for a treat.
Red is a colour I like a lot,
My **Batman** is the best present I ever got.
My favourite person is **Mummy**, who is a gem,
So this, my first poem, is just for them!

Samuel Burch (4)
Teddies Southampton, Southampton

My First Poem

My name is **Jay** and I go to preschool,
My best friend is **Tabby**, who is really cool.
I watch **PAW Patrol** on TV,
Playing **with cars** is lots of fun for me.
I just love **spaghetti** to eat,
And sometimes **cake** for a treat.
Red is a colour I like a lot,
My **big car** is the best present I ever got.
My favourite person is **Mumma**, who is a gem,
So this, my first poem, is just for them!

Jay Salvi (3)
Teddies Southampton, Southampton

My First Poem

My name is Shaeley and I go to preschool,
My best friend is Savvy, who is really cool.
I watch Peppa Pig on TV,
Playing with singing Olaf is lots of fun for me.
I just love carrots to eat,
And sometimes sweeties for a treat.
Pink is a colour I like a lot,
My Peppa Pig toy is the best present I ever got.
My favourite person is Mummy, who is a gem,
So this, my first poem, is just for them!

Shaeley Geddes (3)
Teddies Southampton, Southampton

My First Poem

My name is **Zack** and I go to preschool,
My best friend is **Kaj**, who is really cool.
I watch **Star Wars** on TV,
Playing **an alien game** is lots of fun for me.
I just love **grapes** to eat,
And sometimes **biscuits** for a treat.
Blue is a colour I like a lot,
My **Toy Story talking dolls** are the best present I ever got.
My favourite person is **Daddy**, who is a gem,
So this, my first poem, is just for them!

Zack Day (4)

Teddies Southampton, Southampton

My First Poem

My name is Ava and I go to preschool,
My best friend is Tabby, who is really cool.
I watch Peppa Pig on TV,
Playing cars with Daddy is lots of fun for me.
I just love beans and sausages to eat,
And sometimes a chocolate bar for a treat.
Pink is a colour I like a lot,
My Elsa toy is the best present I ever got.
My favourite person is Mummy, who is a gem,
So this, my first poem, is just for them!

Ava Conway (3)
Teddies Southampton, Southampton

My First Poem

My name is **Sophie** and I go to preschool,
My best friend is **Alissa**, who is really cool.
I watch **Tinker Bell** on TV,
Playing **with my babies** is lots of fun for me.
I just love **bread** to eat,
And sometimes **sweeties** for a treat.
Pink, purple and blue are colours I like a lot,
My **three Elsas** are the best presents I ever got.
My favourite person is **my sister**, who is a gem,
So this, my first poem, is just for them!

Sophie Ulumma-Anusionwu (4)

Teddies Southampton, Southampton

My First Poem

My name is **Isobelle** and I go to preschool,
My best friend is **Emily**, who is really cool.
I watch **Peppa Pig** on TV,
Playing **with my baby brother** is lots of fun for me.
I just love **pasta** to eat,
And sometimes **an apple** for a treat.
Red is a colour I like a lot,
My **new clothes** are the best present I ever got.
My favourite person is **Robyn**, who is a gem,
So this, my first poem, is just for them!

Isobelle Lang (3)
Teddies Southampton, Southampton

My First Poem

My name is Riley and I go to preschool,
My best friend is Alissa, who is really cool.
I watch The Avengers on TV,
Playing bingo is lots of fun for me.
I just love macaroni cheese to eat,
And sometimes sweets for a treat.
Blue is a colour I like a lot,
My Avengers toy is the best present I ever got.
My favourite person is Mummy, who is a gem,
So this, my first poem, is just for them!

Riley Atterbury (4)

Teddies Southampton, Southampton

My First Poem

My name is **Amelia** and I go to preschool,
My best friend is **April**, who is really cool.
I watch **Peppa Pig** on TV,
Playing **the Peppa Pig game** is lots of fun for me.
I just love **spaghetti** to eat,
And sometimes **chocolate** for a treat.
Pink is a colour I like a lot,
My **Elsa doll** is the best present I ever got.
My favourite person is **Charlotte**, who is a gem,
So this, my first poem, is just for them!

Amelia Stone (3)

Teddies Southampton, Southampton

My First Poem

My name is Anoop and I go to preschool,
My best friend is Kaj, who is really cool.
I watch Peppa Pig on TV,
Playing with my camera is lots of fun for me.
I just love pasta to eat,
And sometimes chocolate for a treat.
Green is a colour I like a lot,
My bingo toy is the best present I ever got.
My favourite person is my sister, who is a gem,
So this, my first poem, is just for them!

Anoop Singh (3)
Teddies Southampton, Southampton

My First Poem

My name is Bella and I go to preschool,
My best friend is Isabella, who is really cool.
I watch Frozen on TV,
Playing dollies is lots of fun for me.
I just love pizza to eat,
And sometimes ice cream for a treat.
Purple is a colour I like a lot,
My Peppa Pig is the best present I ever got.
My favourite person is Mummy, who is a gem,
So this, my first poem, is just for them!

Isabella Tang (3)
Teddies Southampton, Southampton

My First Poem

My name is **Alissa** and I go to preschool,
My best friend is **Jack**, who is really cool.
I watch **Go Jetters on the CBeebies Channel** on TV,
Playing **with my dolls** is lots of fun for me.
I just love **spaghetti hoops** to eat,
And sometimes **sweets** for a treat.
Pink is a colour I like a lot,
My **walking, talking and crawling Baby Annabell** is the best present I ever got.
My favourite person is **Mummy**, who is a gem,
So this, my first poem, is just for them!

Alissa Oswald (4)

Teddies Southampton, Southampton

My First Poem

My name is Emily and I go to preschool,
My best friend is Rebecca, who is really cool.
I watch My Little Pony on TV,
Playing the Pig Goes Pop! game is lots of fun for me.
I just love spaghetti to eat,
And sometimes sweets from the sweet shop for a treat.
Pink and purple are colours I like a lot,
My new kitchen toy is the best present I ever got.
My favourite person is Sonia, who is a gem,
So this, my first poem, is just for them!

Emily Grace Mellors (4)
Teddies Southampton, Southampton

My First Poem

My name is **Poppy** and I go to preschool,
My best friend is **Amelia**, who is really cool.
I watch **Peppa Pig** on TV,
Playing **with my pens** is lots of fun for me.
I just love **pasta** to eat,
And sometimes **sweets** for a treat.
Blue is a colour I like a lot,
My **scooter** is the best present I ever got.
My favourite person is **Mummy**, who is a gem,
So this, my first poem, is just for them!

Poppy June Cochrane (3)

Teddies Southampton, Southampton

My First Poem

My name is **Imelda** and I go to preschool,
My best friends are **Ellie and Lucas**, who are really cool.
I watch **The Lion King and The Lion Guard** on TV,
Playing **lions with Nala** is lots of fun for me.
I just love **bread** to eat,
And sometimes **chocolate** for a treat.
Yellow is a colour I like a lot,
My **doggy costume** is the best present I ever got.
My favourite people are **Daddy and Freddy**, who are gems,
So this, my first poem, is just for them!

Imelda Samways (4)
Teddies Southampton, Southampton

My First Poem

My name is Jack and I go to preschool,
My best friend is Alissa, who is really cool.
I watch Star Wars on TV,
Playing snakes and ladders is lots of fun for me.
I just love roast dinner to eat,
And sometimes sweeties for a treat.
Blue and green are colours I like a lot,
My Hulk Smash is the best present I ever got.
My favourite person is Daddy, who is a gem,
So this, my first poem, is just for them!

Jack Moverley (4)

Teddies Southampton, Southampton

My First Poem

My name is **Kaj** and I go to preschool,
My best friend is **Aishik**, who is really cool.
I watch **Bob the Builder** on TV,
Playing **with Transformers** is lots of fun for me.
I just love **roast dinner** to eat,
And sometimes **chocolate** for a treat.
Green, white and pink are colours I like a lot,
My **Gup Launcher** is the best present I ever got.
My favourite person is **Daddy**, who is a gem,
So this, my first poem, is just for them!

Kaj Hill (3)
Teddies Southampton, Southampton

My First Poem

My name is **Jarmal** and I go to preschool,
My best friend is **Daddy**, who is really cool.
I watch **Lightning McQueen** on TV,
Playing **with cars** is lots of fun for me.
I just love **pasta** to eat,
And sometimes **chocolate** for a treat.
Blue is a colour I like a lot,
My **blue car** is the best present I ever got.
My favourite person is **Mummy**, who is a gem,
So this, my first poem, is just for them!

Jarmal Makawa (3)

Teddies Southampton, Southampton

My First Poem

My name is **Esmé** and I go to preschool,
My best friend is **Robyn**, who is really cool.
I watch **CBeebies Prom** on TV,
Playing **with trains** is lots of fun for me.
I just love **spaghetti Bolognese** to eat,
And sometimes **chocolate ice cream** for a treat.
Red is a colour I like a lot,
My **Elsa, Anna, Sven and Olaf** are the best presents I ever got.
My favourite person is **my mummy**, who is a gem,
So this, my first poem, is just for them!

Esmé Dornan (4)
Teddies Southampton, Southampton

My First Poem

My name is **Robyn** and I go to preschool,
My best friend is **Matty**, who is really cool.
I watch **Peppa Pig** on TV,
Playing **with my baby doll** is lots of fun for me.
I just love **macaroni cheese** to eat,
And sometimes **biscuits** for a treat.
Pink is a colour I like a lot,
My **microphone** is the best present I ever got.
My favourite person is **Mummy**, who is a gem,
So this, my first poem, is just for them!

Robyn Hayward (4)

Teddies Southampton, Southampton

My First Poem

My name is **Amelia** and I go to preschool,
My best friends are **Holly and April**, who are really cool.
I watch **Peppa Pig** on TV,
Playing **with Lego** is lots of fun for me.
I just love **pasta** to eat,
And sometimes **sweeties** for a treat.
Pink and purple are colours I like a lot,
My **new bike** is the best present I ever got.
My favourite person is **Gracie**, who is a gem,
So this, my first poem, is just for them!

Amelia Louise Mullins (3)
Teddies Southampton, Southampton

My First Poem

My name is **Zachariya** and I go to preschool,
My best friend is **Zack**, who is really cool.
I watch **Peppa Pig and PAW Patrol** on TV,
Playing **my spider game** is lots of fun for me.
I just love **meatballs and pasta** to eat,
And sometimes **a lollipop** for a treat.
Blue is a colour I like a lot,
My **Star Wars toy** is the best present I ever got.
My favourite person is **Mummy**, who is a gem,
So this, my first poem, is just for them!

Zachariya Uddin (3)

Teddies Southampton, Southampton

My First Poem

My name is Lucas and I go to preschool,
My best friend is Aishik, who is really cool.
I watch PAW Patrol on TV,
Playing football is lots of fun for me.
I just love cereal to eat,
And sometimes chocolate for a treat.
Red and blue are colours I like a lot,
My robot is the best present I ever got.
My favourite people are Mummy and Daddy, who are gems,
So this, my first poem, is just for them!

Lucas William Sargent (4)
Teddies Southampton, Southampton

My First Poem

My name is **Arianna** and I go to preschool,
My best friend is **Tabby**, who is really cool.
I watch **Frozen** on TV,
Playing **Hungry Hippos** is lots of fun for me.
I just love **McDonald's** to eat,
And sometimes **chocolate** for a treat.
Pink is a colour I like a lot,
My **My Little Pony** is the best present I ever got.
My favourite person is **Mummy**, who is a gem,
So this, my first poem, is just for them!

Arianna Gbadamosi (4)

Teddies Southampton, Southampton

My First Poem

My name is **Raiaan** and I go to preschool,
My best friends are **Jawad and Daddy**, who are really cool.
I watch **football** on TV,
Playing **with toys** is lots of fun for me.
I just love **chicken and rice** to eat,
And sometimes **a Kinder egg** for a treat.
Green is a colour I like a lot,
My **Minions** are the best present I ever got.
My favourite people are **Jawad and my dad**, who are gems,
So this, my first poem, is just for them!

Raiaan Rafiq (3)
Tiddlywinks Nursery, Manchester

My First Poem

My name is **Jenson** and I go to preschool,
My best friend is **Bella**, who is really cool.
I watch **Fireman Sam** on TV,
Playing **with the trains** is lots of fun for me.
I just love **crackers** to eat,
And sometimes **chocolate cake** for a treat.
Yellow and black are colours I like a lot,
My **fire engine** is the best present I ever got.
My favourite people are **Mummy and Daddy**, who are gems,
So this, my first poem, is just for them!

Jenson Mansell (4)

Tiddlywinks Nursery, Manchester

My First Poem

My name is **Myla Moo** and I go to preschool,
My best friend is **Erin**, who is really cool.
I watch **Sleeping Beauty** on TV,
Playing **with the doll's house** is lots of fun for me.
I just love **noodles** to eat,
And sometimes **sweeties** for a treat.
Pink is a colour I like a lot,
My **Disney dolls** are the best present I ever got.
My favourite person is **Erin**, who is a gem,
So this, my first poem, is just for them!

Myla Clyne (3)
Tiddlywinks Nursery, Manchester

My First Poem

My name is Erin and I go to preschool,
My best friend is Myla, who is really cool.
I watch Scooby-Doo on TV,
Playing with the bowling balls is lots of fun for me.
I just love fish fingers, mash and beans to eat,
And sometimes ice cream and jelly for a treat.
Pink is a colour I like a lot,
My new sparkling bike is the best present I ever got.
My favourite people are Myla, India and Mummy, who are gems,
So this, my first poem, is just for them!

Erin Thackeray (4)

Tiddlywinks Nursery, Manchester

My First Poem

My name is **Harrison** and I go to preschool,
My best friend is **Mummy**, who is really cool.
I watch **monsters** on TV,
Playing **with Play-Doh** is lots of fun for me.
I just love **mushrooms** to eat,
And sometimes **popcorn** for a treat.
Blue is a colour I like a lot,
My **robot** is the best present I ever got.
My favourite person is **Mummy**, who is a gem,
So this, my first poem, is just for them!

Harrison Fisher (3)

Tiddlywinks Nursery, Manchester

My First Poem

My name is Aniella and I go to preschool,
My best friend is Myla, who is really cool.
I watch Peppa Pig on TV,
Playing with my dolls is lots of fun for me.
I just love fish fingers to eat,
And sometimes banana cake for a treat.
Pink is a colour I like a lot,
My Peppa Pig teddy is the best present I ever got.
My favourite person is Daddy, who is a gem,
So this, my first poem, is just for them!

Aniella Dalbin (3)

Tiddlywinks Nursery, Manchester

My First Poem

My name is **Kale** and I go to preschool,
My best friend is **Maisie**, who is really cool.
I watch **Fireman Sam** on TV,
Playing **on my bike** is lots of fun for me.
I just love **pasta** to eat,
And sometimes **cake** for a treat.
Green is a colour I like a lot,
My **teddy bear** is the best present I ever got.
My favourite person is **Maisie**, who is a gem,
So this, my first poem, is just for them!

Kale Lamey-McArthur (3)
Tiddlywinks Nursery, Manchester

My First Poem

My name is Eva and I go to preschool,
My best friend is Keane, who is really cool.
I watch PAW Patrol on TV,
Playing trains is lots of fun for me.
I just love bananas to eat,
And sometimes chocolate for a treat.
Yellow is a colour I like a lot,
My Spider-Man is the best present I ever got.
My favourite person is Keane, who is a gem,
So this, my first poem, is just for them!

Eva Walklett (3)

Tiddlywinks Nursery, Manchester

My First Poem

My name is **Eric** and I go to preschool,
My best friend is **Myla**, who is really cool.
I watch **Batman** on TV,
Playing **diggers** is lots of fun for me.
I just love **strawberry ice cream** to eat,
And sometimes **chocolate** for a treat.
Blue is a colour I like a lot,
My **digger** is the best present I ever got.
My favourite person is **Mummy**, who is a gem,
So this, my first poem, is just for them!

Eric McCormick (3)

Tiddlywinks Nursery, Manchester

My First Poem

We hope you have enjoyed reading this book – and that you will continue to enjoy it in the coming years.

If you're a young writer who enjoys reading and creative writing, or the parent of an enthusiastic poet or story writer, do visit our websites, www.myfirstpoem.com and www.youngwriters.co.uk. Here you will find free competitions, workshops and games, as well as recommended reads, a poetry glossary and our blog.

If you would like to order further copies of this book, or any of our other titles, then please give us a call or visit www.myfirstpoem.com.

My First Poem
Remus House
Coltsfoot Drive
Peterborough
PE2 9BF

Tel: 01733 898110
info@myfirstpoem.com